Sherlock Holmes
and the
Disgraced Inspector

John Hall

First published in 1998 by
Breese Books
This revised edition published in 2020 by
Baker Street Studios Ltd and
The Irregular Special Press for
Breese Books
Endeavour House
170 Woodland Road, Sawston
Cambridge, CB22 3DX, UK

ISBN: 978 0 947533 88 5

Cover Illustration: New Scotland Yard from an 1890 postcard of London.

Typeset in 8/11/20pt Palatino

BY THE SAME AUTHOR

SHERLOCK HOLMES AND THE ABBEY SCHOOL MYSTERY
SHERLOCK HOLMES AND THE ADLER PAPERS
SHERLOCK HOLMES AND THE BOULEVARD ASSASSIN
SHERLOCK HOLMES AND THE FRIGHTENED CHAMBERMAID
SHERLOCK HOLMES AND THE HAMMERFORD WILL
SHERLOCK HOLMES AT THE RAFFLES HOTEL
SHERLOCK HOLMES AND THE TELEPHONE MURDER MYSTERY
SPECIAL COMMISSION
THE TRAVELS OF SHERLOCK HOLMES

One

As what I might term the official biographer of Mr Sherlock Holmes, I have perforce been obliged to become accustomed to being asked a good many questions about the world's greatest, if not actually first, consulting detective. A great many of these questions are trivial and some are nothing more than impertinent, but some are more serious, and there are some which are perennial, questions which almost everyone asks. One of these latter evergreen questions, couched in various terms, concerns the relationship between Sherlock Holmes and Inspector Lestrade of Scotland Yard. 'When we first hear of Lestrade,' say these hypothetical enquirers in effect, 'he is consulting Holmes several times a week over a forgery case; for many years he then both consults Holmes and rejects his advice; finally, he regards Holmes almost with adulation.'

In fact, there is no great mystery about any of this. When I first met Holmes, he was at the very start of his career. Indeed, it is no insult to say that in those days he was in very truth nothing much more than a consulting detective, an armchair reasoner, rather than a man of action. Lestrade could ask Holmes's opinion, and Holmes could draw upon his own extensive knowledge of the history of crime to give that opinion, without either man treading, as it were, upon the other's toes, encroaching into the province which belonged more correctly to his fellow.

Later, when Holmes left his armchair, a development for which I myself might perhaps venture to claim a modest share of credit, then he and Lestrade were brought into more or less direct personal conflict. It was not that Lestrade did not value Holmes's opinion. Rather it was that Lestrade could not in all conscience be seen to consult Holmes too often, or listen to his advice in every case, for that would merely have made Lestrade look inept in the eyes of his superiors. Lestrade was thus in the somewhat unenviable position of needing Holmes's help on many occasions, whilst still being obliged to try to maintain his own position at Scotland Yard. You must remember that at this time there was a good deal of rivalry between the various policemen; I seem to recall that I have mentioned elsewhere the jealousy which existed between Lestrade and his colleague Gregson right at the very start of my acquaintance with Holmes.

Now we come to the last point, the fact that Lestrade came to have a genuine admiration for Holmes. In part, and it was a very large part, this was nothing more than the effect of time, Lestrade having had so many proofs of Holmes's ability that he could not help but rely upon him and admire him. But that was not the whole story. There was more, a specific instance when Lestrade desperately needed help, and Holmes came to his assistance. I have never revealed this fact before, and indeed, were it not for events which I need not dwell upon, I should not be telling the tale even now.

It was, then, a dull October day a year or so after Holmes had returned to London. I was living at 221B Baker Street, and we had more or less resumed the old partnership on the old terms. We had finished breakfast a long hour ago, but neither of us had much inclination to be out and about. Holmes was curled up in an armchair reading a little black-letter volume he had just acquired, *The Burnynge of Paules Church* by the Bishop of Durham, if memory serves me correctly, and saying nothing, other than making an occasional bitter remark as to the destiny which ultimately awaits those who mutilate old books by cutting out ornate capitals. For myself, even reading seemed too active, and I was whiling away the time standing in the bow window and idly regarding the passing throng.

After a time, I turned to Holmes. 'You once said something to the effect that a maiden vacillating upon the pavement betokened an affair of the heart,' said I.

'Did I?' he answered without looking up from the page. 'It seems a damned silly thing to say, but I have no doubt that you are correct.' He suddenly looked up at me, and threw the book down. 'But is there a maiden vacillating, then? Have we a case, think you?'

'No maiden, certainly, whether vacillating or otherwise,' said I with a laugh. 'I should be underestimating Lestrade to say that. But he is certainly showing every sign of indecision.'

'What, Lestrade?' Holmes's interest was stirred, I could tell.

'Yes.' I nodded at the window. 'He is standing over the road, by the doorway of Camden House, and looking across here. He has looked three times at the front door, and four or five times has he glanced up at this window. The last time he caught sight of me, and turned away rather pointedly. But he is still there.'

'Now, that is indeed interesting.' Holmes left his chair and came over to my side. 'Yes,' he said, 'it is he.' There could indeed be no mistaking Inspector Lestrade's wiry figure, or his sharp, alert features. 'Now, I wonder just what he is up to?' Holmes mused, then fell silent.

'Yes, one does ...' I began, turning to Holmes. But he was gone. I looked across the room to see him changing his dressing gown for an overcoat. He came back to the window and stared out. 'Still vacillating, is he? Another moment, I think, Watson, and he will be away. Yes, by Jove, he is off. But I shall have him, Doctor! Stay here, if you will, and I shall bring him up to give us a full explanation.'

Before I could think of anything by way of reply, Holmes was out of the room, snatching his hat from the peg as he passed it. I stood there, mystified, looking at the little drama that unfolded.

As I have said, Lestrade, after standing on the opposite pavement looking across at 221B for some considerable time, had suddenly squared his shoulders for all the world as if he had finally come to a decision, turned on his heel, and set off down Baker Street. He did not hasten; but Holmes, who had just emerged from our front door, did. He fairly ran across the road and after Lestrade, slowing down when he was about ten paces from the detective, and strolling to catch up with him in the most casual manner possible.

I saw Holmes tap Lestrade on the shoulder with the crook of his stick, to get his attention; I saw the Scotland Yard man start, and turn, and look surprised to see Holmes. There followed a short conversation, at the end of which Holmes took Lestrade by the arm in what was obviously a friendly but firm fashion, and led him back to our front door.

Determined not to spoil Holmes's little theatrical performance, I hastily settled myself in the chair he had vacated, and began reading a novel. As the door opened, and I heard Holmes's somewhat strident tones inviting Lestrade to step inside, I glanced up, as if surprised to see them. 'Good morning, Inspector,' said I. 'Take a seat. Shall I ring and ask Mrs Hudson for a pot of tea, or is it too early in the day for something stronger?'

'Brandy,' said Lestrade shortly, throwing himself into a chair. 'That is, if it's not troubling you too much?'

'No trouble at all,' said Holmes, busying himself with the decanter and gasogene. 'Watson?'

'Bad form to let a guest drink alone, Holmes. Only a small one, though,' I added, 'for it is rather early.'

Holmes, I regret to say, took me at my word. I lifted my glass to the light in an attempt to determine whether he had indeed dispensed a drop of the spirit, albeit a pathetically parsimonious drop, and, looking through the thin glass of the balloon, was astounded to see Lestrade drain his far more generous measure at a single gulp.

'Another, Lestrade?' asked Holmes, with just a hint of cynicism in his tone.

Lestrade set his glass down, and wiped his lips with the back of a rather unsteady hand. 'Not at the moment, Mr Holmes,' said he. 'As Doctor Watson says, it is a bit early in the day.' He gave a sort of uneasy laugh, and went on, 'The fact is, gentlemen, I'm rather ashamed that you should see me like this. The brandy, and all. It's ... that is to say ... well, I've had what you might call a nasty turn.'

'Indeed?' said I. 'If I can be of professional assistance, pray do not hesitate to say so.'

Lestrade shook his head. 'It's nothing in your line, Doctor,' he told me. He glanced sidelong at Holmes. 'No, it's more ...' and he fell silent.

Holmes, who had been hanging up his coat and hat and resuming his old dressing gown, sat down opposite Lestrade. 'Command me, Lestrade,' said he.

'Indeed, yes,' I echoed.

Lestrade gave another embarrassed laugh. 'It's kind of you, Mr Holmes. And you too, Doctor. But even you, gents, for all your cleverness, could hardly be expected to help me now. And then, if you did, I hardly like to think of the consequences.' He collected himself with an obvious effort. 'Well, to be plain, gentlemen, you would merely be sharing in my disgrace. And that to no useful purpose, for I see no way out of it, and that's a fact.'

'Disgrace?' said I.

Holmes sat back in his chair, and regarded the detective critically. 'You are like Watson,' said he, 'telling your tale back to front, with the ending first. I know you do not drink through the day, save, perhaps, in some dire extremity such as the present instance. You are happily married, and thus proof against the charms of mistress, maid and housekeeper alike.' Lestrade gave a sardonic and perhaps a slightly regretful grin at this. 'Moreover,' Holmes continued, 'you are one of those sea-green incorruptibles of whom someone or the other once wrote in such glowing terms. There is therefore no great difficulty in deducing that it is a question of some professional difficulty, a delicate matter of professional conduct, which has brought you to the sorry state of sitting by our fireside to drink brandy and soda at half past ten in the morning.' He leaned forward and regarded Lestrade keenly. 'Or perhaps it might be more accurate to term it suspected professional misconduct?'

Lestrade smiled weakly. 'There's no fooling you, sir,' said he, then he fell silent again.

Holmes put the tips of his fingers together, and regarded the ceiling. 'It may perhaps have been the case,' said he, choosing his words with evident care, 'that I have had occasion in the past to point out certain deficiencies in your deductive technique. However, that was done, I assure you, in no carping or unfriendly spirit. For straightforward police work, you are unequalled. In fact, were I an ordinary, unimaginative villain there is no hand that I would less like to feel on my collar than that of Inspector Lestrade.'

Lestrade took a moment to work this out. 'Why, thank you, Mr Holmes,' said he, cheering up somewhat.

'And that being the case,' said I, 'will you not tell us your troubles? Even if we cannot help, we can at least lend a sympathetic ear. A trouble shared is a trouble halved, you know.'

'Watson is right, as usual,' said Holmes. 'Help yourself to a cigar,' he added. 'And perhaps another brandy?'

'Well, a small one, then, but only if Doctor Watson is having one.'

'Oh, certainly, certainly. Anything to help.'

Holmes frowned. 'It were as well to keep a clear head,' said he.

'Not much chance of anything else!' said I, gazing ruefully at the niggardly measure he had poured.

He affected not to have heard me. 'Now, Lestrade,' he said, 'you mentioned "disgrace", I think?'

'Complete and utter disgrace, sir,' agreed Lestrade, nodding his head.

'Tell us about it,' ordered Holmes.

Lestrade rubbed his head. 'I don't really know where to begin, Mr Holmes.'

'At the beginning, man.'

Lestrade put his glass down, and lit a cigar. 'You were right about keeping a clear head,' said he, 'so I won't have any more brandy, but I'd be grateful for a glass of water by my side, for my tale is a long one, and perhaps will be somewhat confused.

It began,' he went on, 'some three weeks ago, or the first part of it did anyway. Or did it perhaps begin twenty years ago?'

Holmes looked sternly at him. 'Which is it, Lestrade? Three weeks, or twenty years?'

'Well,' said Lestrade, 'it's better if we start with the three week business, as being nearer, as it were, and thus easier to recollect. Three weeks ago, then, I was called to investigate a robbery and brutal murder at the town house of Sir Octavius Fotheringay.'

Holmes raised an eyebrow.

'Name means something, Mr Holmes?' asked Lestrade with a quizzical look.

'It sounds as if it should, but I cannot quite recollect the details. No matter,' said Holmes, 'continue with your tale, Lestrade, for I can always look him up in my index should he continue to elude me.'

'Oh, he'll come to mind soon enough,' said Lestrade, with the closest approach to humour that I had seen in him since he sat down.

'The name means nothing to me,' said I, endeavouring to emulate Holmes's methods, 'but I take it he was a self-made man?'

'Why that?' asked Holmes curiously.

'Elementary, my dear Holmes! If he were the eighth child, as his name suggests, and if his father were a baronet, which is the only hereditary rank entitling his eldest son to be "Sir" somebody-or-other, then it would be most improbable for the first seven children to be all girls. The inescapable conclusion is surely that he earned his knighthood himself.'

'Well done, Watson! Inescapable, Lestrade?'

'Maybe it is, but it's wrong,' said Lestrade. 'He's a baronet, all right. Inherited from his elder brother. Or one of 'em.'

'Oh?' Holmes looked a question.

Lestrade leaned forward in his chair and looked intently at us. 'Eight in the family, and this Octavius the last, exactly as Doctor Watson deduced. Five girls, three boys. The oldest brother died young, in mysterious circumstances. Out riding

11

with this Octavius, nobody else about, and his horse, an old, well-mannered horse, mark you, throws him.'

'Riding accident, then?' said I. 'Might happen to anybody. I recall one time in Jalalabad ...'

'Riding accident my foot!' said Lestrade coarsely. 'He'd been raised with horses, rode a pony at three, a horse from being four or five. Why, he was like one of them old Greek chaps, centurions, was it? Half man, and half horse. This was out in the country, of course, and the local police handled it. That is, if you can call it "handling" it. We never got a look in, the Yard, I mean. If we had ... well! But let's be kind and leave that for the moment. A year or so later, the father dies. Natural causes that time, no doubt of that, and the second son inherits the title. A year or so after that, the eldest son announces his engagement. A fortnight later, blow me if he doesn't die too. Left the gas on in his bedroom, unlit, if you'll believe it. That was here in London, and you can be sure we investigated it pretty thoroughly.'

'And?'

Lestrade shrugged. 'And nothing. This Octavius was nowhere near the family's town house, or so it appeared. He was in Brighton, with a lady, if that's what you could call her. Plenty of witnesses, at the hotel and what have you, so it was iron-clad. But I had my eye on him, Mr Holmes.'

'You were right to do so, for it sounds most suspicious. I recollect the last case, now you mention it. Some five or six years back?'

'Getting on for ten,' amended Lestrade.

'Is that so? Ah, me.' Holmes sat up straight and looked keenly at Lestrade. 'The case was never resolved, there were no suspects at all, is that not so?'

Lestrade nodded. 'None, apart from the obvious. No, sir. Still open, Mr Holmes. Well, a week back, I was called to the town house, now the property of Sir Octavius, for a second time. Place had been robbed, turned upside down, and his wife lying dead amongst it all. A bad business, a cruel business. Head bashed in. And it wasn't as if she could have been much danger to any determined burglar, for the poor lady was practically an invalid.'

'A bit too much of a coincidence, that,' said I.

'Even Watson, most tolerant of men, cannot accept that it is a coincidence,' Holmes told Lestrade. 'I saw the reports of that, of course, although I was not personally consulted.' He looked a question.

The Scotland Yard man shook his head sadly. 'Nothing to be made of it, sir,' said he. 'Once again, Sir Octavius had an unshakeable alibi. He was with his lawyer.' And he hesitated.

'Well?'

'Well, Mr Holmes, you'll have difficulty believing this, but a few years back this lawyer's wife died in exactly the same way. Killed in the course of a robbery.'

'Now, that really is lightning striking twice, or indeed three times, in the same place!' I exclaimed. 'Not merely a coincidence, but a coincidence of truly monumental, unbelievable, proportions.'

Lestrade nodded. 'So I thought, Doctor, you may be sure. I picked up Sir Octavius, and the lawyer chap, and laid into them both pretty well.' He broke off, and mopped his brow.

'Well?' asked Holmes again.

'I wish to Heaven I may never have such an interview a second time,' said Lestrade. 'The lawyer chap, he's done well for himself, Queen's Counsel now, and tipped to become a judge in the not too distant future. "How dare I, a mere vulgar policeman, suggest anything of that kind?", says he, and so on and so forth. Then when he ran out of steam, Sir Octavius got started. "Grief-stricken, heart-broken, how dare I ..." and off we went down the same road. Ending with, "The Police Commissioner and the Home Secretary shall hear of this!", and I don't know what else.'

It was my turn to ask, 'Well?'

'Well, Doctor, the commissioner did hear of it. I was summoned to appear before the assistant commissioner a couple of days ago, and had another most unpleasant half hour.'

'I fail to see the reason for any unpleasantness, Lestrade,' said I. 'Even if the fellow's alibi was unshakeable, the string of curious events, be they coincidence or no, surely made him an obvious suspect? You would have been remiss indeed had you not questioned him pretty closely.'

'Ah, Doctor, these fellows stick together from school onwards,' said Lestrade. 'Anyway, the upshot was that I was instructed to leave poor Sir Octavius to grieve in peace, and get out and look for a gang of robbers.'

'What reason had he for killing his wife?' asked Holmes.

'Money,' said Lestrade. 'By all accounts, Sir Octavius had blown his own inheritance, and such money as there was came from his wife. He couldn't sell the house, for that is entailed.'

'Ah.'

'Then the wife was insured, and for a hefty amount. And the stuff that was stolen was all hers to boot, jewellery and silver and what have you.'

'I see,' said Holmes.

'I suspect he'd had his eye on that for some time, as representing a way out of his troubles,' Lestrade continued, 'but of course it would be awkward trying to pinch the goods with his wife still there to see. Dead wives don't nag.'

'Or talk to their fathers, or brothers, or lawyers, or the police,' I added.

'Indeed not,' said Lestrade. 'And for good measure, Sir Octavius is now free to marry another rich woman, of he finds one daft enough. Oh, there's plenty of motives, Mr Holmes, it's just a matter of picking the right one. Or two.'

'H'mm. But further investigation has, you say, been firmly ruled out?'

'Very firmly, sir,' said Lestrade with a rueful grin.

'I may be able to look at that matter myself,' said Holmes thoughtfully. 'But I cannot see that this business is any reason for distress on your part. You have had reverses enough in your time … as I have myself,' he added rather hastily, 'and I cannot see that one uncomfortable interview with your chief is cause for the condition you appear to be in.'

'If that were all, if it were that and nothing more,' said Lestrade, 'I'd grin and bear it. Part of the job, as you say. But it isn't all, Mr Holmes. Not by a long chalk. As I say, that was a couple of days ago, and the fuss was just starting to die a natural death, so to speak, when this other business happened.'

'And what was that?'

Lestrade mopped his brow. 'It all began, you might say, some twenty years ago, before ever I met you, Mr Holmes, or you, Doctor.' He took a sip of water. 'In those days I was a young detective sergeant, and keen as mustard. There was me and Toby Gregson, both joined the force at the same time, both made detective at the same time, then sergeant. Not that Toby has anything to do with it, other than the fact that there was a bit of rivalry between us, friendly rivalry. More or less friendly. It kept us both on our toes, eager to please our superiors, eager to make it to inspector.

'Anyway, you don't want to know about all that, other than that I was keen as mustard to get on, make my name. There was a big case came up, a nasty case, very nasty. Made the headlines in all the newspapers at the time.' He took another sip from the glass of water which Holmes had given him. 'Very nasty,' he repeated. 'Five young boys, all of them disappeared, and the families distraught. Maybe six, because one went about three, four months before the others. Then five went more or less together, one, two, three, regular as clockwork, one a month, and all around the time of the full moon.'

'A lunatic?' I suggested.

Lestrade shrugged. 'That was one theory, and a popular theory, too, Doctor, yes, the intervals between them being as regular as they were. Or devil-worship, or ghosts, or I don't know what, was suggested by fanciful folk with nothing better to do than dream up nonsense. Of course, you can imagine the sort of things they were thinking down in the East End, where the boys lived, or had lived. Some of the women there were going frantic, wondering if their kiddy might be next.'

Holmes nodded. 'Once again, I have some recollection of the case,' said he, 'although I was not living in London at the time.'

'Before your time, sir, like I said,' agreed Lestrade. 'Anyway, I was put on to the case, or to be accurate, Inspector White was put on to it, and I was his sergeant. Old "Chalky" White,' he added. 'Of course, nobody called him "Chalky" to his face, you understand. The man really in charge of the case was Buller, Superintendent Buller, he's dead, now. Well, the newspapers made a big thing of it, as I say, and as you can readily imagine, and one day Buller comes in white as a sheet. He'd been called in for a little friendly chat with the assistant commissioner, who'd had a little chat of his own with the Home Secretary. You can guess the rest. "Chalky" got an earful, and he gave me an earful, said we must have an early arrest, and so on. Well, there we were, urged ... no, ordered, to do something, and fast; and at the same time, I was anxious to make a good showing, for my own career.'

'And you made an honest mistake?' I suggested.

Lestrade shook his head impatiently. 'The devil I did! No, Doctor, hear me out, if you will, for it's a complicated story. We hadn't got the ghost of a clue ...'

Holmes seemed about to speak, and Lestrade looked at him. Holmes waved a hand in a languid fashion, to indicate that the inspector should continue.

'We hadn't the ghost of a clue,' said Lestrade firmly, 'and I honestly believe that you wouldn't have had one either, sir. The boys had nothing in common, other than living in London. Four were East End lads, poor but honest, as the newspapers put it, one was better off, a bit, from a fairly well to do background in trade, a little shop in Clerkenwell, his father had, and the first one, the one we weren't sure about, his father was Sir somebody or the other. The mother, she was a real lady, heart-broken she was, you could see that.'

'And he lived where?'

'Out Twickenham way. Different from the others, you see, for they were all more or less from the one small area, East End, as I say, and then there was a gap between him and the rest, so we thought it was completely different, the first one. Unrelated. Anyway, there we were, pretty well at our wits' end, when we got this letter.'

'Anonymous?'

Lestrade nodded. 'Although we did think it was his next-door neighbour. In any event, that's neither here nor there, who sent it. The important thing was that it concerned a man called Jacobson. Said he'd been in and out at all sorts of odd hours, that he was strange, the usual stuff and nonsense. A case like that, you get all sorts of things, people confessing to things they couldn't have done, or denouncing their neighbours. This Jacobson was strange, that was right enough, and I'll tell you about that in a moment. And maybe it was that, or maybe it was his name, foreign-sounding as it was. Although in fact he was as English as you or me,' added Lestrade without the slightest trace of irony. 'Well, Buller said, what the ... you know ... we'd talked to dozens, maybe hundreds, of men, it won't hurt to talk to this one as well.' He paused, and took another sip of water. 'Don't get me wrong, gents. I'm perhaps making it sound more important than it seemed at the time. As I say, with a case like that, you know how it is. You'll get a couple of nasty letters pretty well every morning, saying that so-and-so's up to no good, that sort of thing. Buller just shrugged his shoulders when he saw this letter, said bring him along to the station, have a word, that sort of thing, routine, you might say. So we did.'

'And?' asked Holmes.

'And he told us that he'd done it.'

'As simple as that?' said I, incredulous.

Lestrade nodded. 'As simple as that, very nearly, Doctor. I went along and picked him up. They didn't think it was important enough to go there themselves, the superintendent and the inspector, you see. That's how little they thought of it. He was only a youngish chap, twenty-three, or four, and he seemed very nervous when I asked him to go along of me. Well, that's neither here nor there, for there's many an innocent man acts odd, for all the world as if he was guilty, when the police stop him. So, I took him to the station, and put him in a cell, while I went to fetch Inspector White. When we walked in, this Jacobson practically broke down in tears, said he'd been kept awake at nights thinking about what he'd done, that sort of

17

thing. I've seen some rum things in my day but that beat all. Why, I almost felt ashamed for him.'

'And he admitted what, exactly?' said Holmes.

'Murder, sir. Abduction and murder. Five murders, to be exact.'

'Five? Not six?'

Lestrade shook his head. 'Not the first one, he denied all knowledge of that. Well, that was fair enough, we'd thought that was different, like I said.'

'You are certain it was unconnected with the others?' asked Holmes.

'Certain as can be, sir. You'd perhaps be surprised just how easy it is to disappear in London, and how many people do vanish every year. Of course, mostly they're husbands wanting to skip out on their wives, and that kind of thing, but there are lots of homeless children in this fair city. Some find a niche, somehow, some do come to a sticky end, but this case was so regular, so consistent, like, a real pattern to it, the regular disappearances and all. That's what drew our attention to it, for in the ordinary way a missing child would just be reported to the local station, and they'd do what they could.' He sighed. 'Now, I was talking of Jacobson. Well, Chalky asks him, "Very well my lad, where's the bodies?" And he told us where one … and only one, mark you … of 'em was.' He cleared his throat. 'Well, Chalky kept on at him, saying you must know, if you did 'em in, that kind of thing, so where are the other four? And after a time, and a good long time it was too, this Jacobson says something like, "No, it was Algy who was driving", or words to that effect, "I didn't see where we were going", says he.'

'Algy?' asked Holmes, sitting up.

'All in good time, Mr Holmes,' said Lestrade. 'Well, you can imagine that we pretty well laid into him then, asked him who's Algy, where's he live, what has he to do with it, all that kind of thing. And would you believe this Jacobson wouldn't tell us? Seemed for all the world as if he regretted having blurted the name out, and was damned if he'd say any more. Well, this went on for maybe two, three, hours. Wouldn't say another word, only that he deserved to hang for what he'd done. Said that more than once, loud and clear. Then Chalky ... he was the inspector, remember, and I was only his sergeant ... he looks at me, and he winks, and he says, "Shove off, lad, and get yourself a cup of tea".'

'And?'

'And I did,' said Lestrade, with some considerable embarrassment. He coughed, and studied his boots.

'Yes?'

'And when I went back, Jacobson was snivelling, and he had a black eye, and his nose was bleeding.'

'Ah. I see.'

'But he had told Chalky that the other bloke was an Algernon Clayton,' said Lestrade.

'Do I understand you to say that this ... Inspector White, was it ... had more or less beaten the information out of this suspect?' I asked, with some surprise.

Lestrade gave an odd shrug of his shoulders. 'You know how it is, Doctor,' he said defensively. 'Some of these old lags are tough, and if you didn't use the back of your hand or the toe of your boot occasionally ...' and he ended the sentiment with another shrug.

'In ancient China,' said Holmes, 'the judges could not pass sentence without a confession, and to prevent hardened criminals remaining silent the courts were empowered to use torture in moderation.'

'There you are,' said Lestrade. 'If the old emperors and typhoons and what-have-you needed a bit of rough stuff now and then, I'm sure we do.'

'With a hardened criminal, perhaps,' said I. 'Although even then, not everyone would agree that it is entirely necessary. But this young man was not, as I understand you, a hardened criminal? You have said yourself that he was not originally even suspected of this crime.'

Lestrade had the grace to look embarrassed. 'That's maybe true,' said he, 'but under the circumstances it didn't seem that way to me then. And, as I say, he confessed. What more could you ask for, Doctor?'

'And you arrested this Clayton?' asked Holmes.

19

'We did. And he denied the whole thing. Said he'd no sort of alibi, that he'd been out working when the lads vanished. Turned out he was a cab driver, by the way.'

'Which accounts for the other fellow saying that Clayton had been driving?'

Lestrade nodded. 'But you're making me do what you complained of, sir, and tell my tale out of order. We didn't just take this Jacobson's word for it that Clayton was involved. We set a man to keep an eye on him, Clayton that is, while we made Jacobson lead us to where he, or they, as the case might be, had hidden the body he'd spoken of.' He stopped, and indicated his glass. 'If I might have just the merest splash of brandy, Doctor? Thank you. I'll never forget that lad,' he went on. 'He was buried on a bit of waste ground by the river. What they'd done to him ...' and he shuddered, and drank his brandy.

'Was there any unpleasantness, any assault?' I asked, with some distaste.

'Not unless you count being cut up like cats' meat,' said Lestrade shortly. He recovered his composure, and gave an uneasy smile. 'I'm sorry, Doctor. No, I know well enough what you mean. No, sir, there was no unpleasantness of that kind. Not that there needed to be. It was bad enough as it was, Lord knows.'

'But might there have been?' Holmes wanted to know. 'Were any of these boys of doubtful repute in that respect?'

'Not a bit of it, sir,' Lestrade told him. 'I know what you're driving at. Some of these youngsters, boys or girls, a couple of shillings and they're anybody's, and if they get more than they bargained for, well, we all say "How terrible!", and so it is, but I don't know as how they haven't mostly just themselves to blame. But there was nothing of that kind in this case, I'll swear to that. The youngest was only six, the oldest twelve or thirteen. A couple of them had little jobs, the others were at school, poor little beggars. Nothing special about any of 'em, none of them were plaster saints, but to end up like mutton on a butcher's slab ...' and he shuddered visibly.

I passed the decanter over to him. 'Help yourself,' I told him, 'for the recollection is evidently a painful one.'

'It is, Doctor, and that's a fact. Chalky White had seen pretty well everything, hard as nails, Chalky, and even he was turned over by it all. Well, to cut a long story short, once we'd found the body, and knew that Jacobson had told us the truth, or at any rate, a part of it, then naturally we arrested Clayton.' He poured himself more brandy. 'Algernon Clayton. Now, he really was a queer fish if you like. Even odder than Jacobson, if you ask me. Cold, not showing any sort of emotion, neither guilt, nor remorse, nor anger. Nothing. Well, we'd got the body, and we'd got Jacobson's confession, so we fairly went for Clayton.'

'And you say he denied it?' asked Holmes.

'Yes, sir. Denied the whole thing, flatly.'

'And did Inspector White use the same investigative technique as he had used on Jacobson?'

Lestrade flushed. 'By then, Buller had taken over the case, more or less, and he took charge of the questioning. It was all above board with him, I can tell you. Buller made Clayton look at the body we'd found. "What d'you say to that?" Buller asks him. And Clayton says, "Terrible. Tragic. But absolutely nothing to do with me", he says.'

'And when you read Jacobson's confession to him?'

'Still denied it. "He's lying", he says, "or else he's making a mistake", and that was all he said about that. He hadn't any sort of alibi, I told you that, just said that he'd been out driving his cab, and stuck to that. Most of the lads had vanished in the evening, didn't get home from work or school, that sort of thing. Clayton couldn't produce any witnesses who'd been with him when the boys vanished ...'

'No passengers?'

'Who remembers a cab driver, Mr Holmes? But, by the same token, we couldn't find any witnesses who put him, or his cab, or indeed any cab, anywhere that could be useful to us. Part of the difficulty was, we didn't have the other bodies, so we didn't really know where to look for anyone who might possibly have witnessed their being disposed of.'

'But the case went to court, on the strength of Jacobson's confession?'

'It did, sir. The confession counted for a good deal, and you could tell that just looking at the jury. That, and the photographs they were shown of the body.'

'And Clayton continued to maintain his innocence at the trial?' I asked.

'He did. The prosecution made a big thing of the body, said what did Clayton say to that? He just repeated what he'd already told us, said it was an awful thing, but nothing to do with him. We had a body, fair enough, but we also had Jacobson's confession, so why involve him, Clayton that is? His lawyer made that point very strongly.'

'But to no avail?' asked Holmes.

'The thing was,' said Lestrade, 'we knew Jacobson had killed the one lad, because the body was where he'd said it was. So that was certain. In fact, it was about the only certain thing in the whole sorry business. Now, if he'd told the truth about that, then why should he lie about the rest? Why should he lie as to Clayton's being involved? That's what did for Clayton. The jury didn't take above half an hour. Guilty, the pair of them. And both sentenced to hang. But there was something, some doubt in the judge's mind, or an appeal, perhaps, and the sentences were both altered to penal servitude for life.'

Holmes nodded. 'That seems ... I beg your pardon, Lestrade. Please go on.'

'This was, what, twenty years ago? More. About ten years back, there was a bit of a fuss, some newspaper took up the cudgels on behalf of Clayton, said it was wrong to lock him up, the usual thing. And one or two prominent men took up the same cry. Then after a year or so, they persuaded the Home Secretary to offer Clayton a pardon. Not the other one, Jacobson, though, because everybody knew he was guilty, of course.'

'Ah,' said Holmes, 'I do remember that. Clayton refused the pardon, did he not?'

'He did.'

'Why on earth should he refuse a pardon?' I asked, puzzled. 'I should have thought that he would grab at it with both hands.'

'He said that a pardon was just that, that it meant that he'd committed the crime all right, but was being pardoned for it, excused, let off,' said Lestrade. 'And he said no, he hadn't committed any crime, so he didn't need pardoning, thank you very much. His supporters stuck at it, and they took the matter up with every court that would listen to them. That part of it didn't make any headlines, of course, it was all lawyers' stuff, writs, and petitions, and appeals, and what-have-you. But they kept at it, from one place to another, for about five years, now.' He drank more brandy.

'And?' asked Holmes.

'And yesterday the Lords of Appeal set the verdict aside. Clayton is free as a bird, and innocent as a new-born babe.'

I leaned forward and looked at him, puzzled. 'Can they do that?' I asked.

'They can,' said Lestrade. 'It's not an everyday thing, for it's unusual, and it's complicated, and it rocks the legal boat, so to speak, and so it doesn't often happen, but it can be done.'

'And it is naturally a very considerable shock to you,' said Holmes gently.

'It is a great deal more than that, sir,' said Lestrade grimly. 'For I have been suspended from duty. And I know that this is only the beginning. I am done, Mr Holmes. Disgraced. Finished. Ruined, completely and utterly!'

Two

'Come now, Lestrade,' said Holmes. 'I feel that you are overstating the gravity of the situation. We are all human, we all make mistakes. Why, even I myself have had my failures, though mercifully few and far between.'

Lestrade shook his head. 'With all possible respect, Mr Holmes, you did not talk to my superintendent this morning, and I did. Bad news travels fast, they say, and the duty inspector told me the outcome of the court hearing when I first set foot in the station this morning, and he also told me that the superintendent would like to see me. I knew what that was about, of course. Anyway, I goes along to his room, and he sits me down, asks have I heard about the appeal? I say, yes. He hums and haws, and then gets down to business.'

"There'll be a fuss and a half about this, Lestrade", says he. I agree with him. "That being the case", he goes on, "it might be as well to consider our position". I ask you, "our" position! He's safe enough, whatever happens. "Clayton is already talking about suing the police for kidnap and wrongful arrest and I don't know what else", he tells me.

'"Can he do that?" I asked him. He sort of looks at me, and he says, careful like, "I'm not sure about the police, as being part of the Crown, and so immune, although that's for the lawyers to argue about. But he can take action against an individual officer". Ohoh, I tells myself, so that's it, is it? "And that being the case", says he, "we don't want to attract

attract attention to ourselves, do we?" I must 'ave looked blank, as well I might, for I didn't know what the devil he was talking about. He sighs. "There'll have to be an enquiry, of course", he tells me.

'"I suppose there will, sir", says I.

'"Of course," says he, "if the officer concerned wasn't an officer at the time of any enquiry, that might be different. Do you follow?"

'Well, I can't have looked any less blank at that. He sighs again, and says, "How would you feel about retiring? Take your pension, for you're not getting any younger, after all, buy a nice little pub out in the country, forget all about Clayton, and the rest of the bunch. How's that sound?"

'Well, it sounded grand, has done for a few years now, to be honest, but I wasn't telling him that. Not when it was put to me in those terms, gents. "Would you go, sir, with your tail between your legs?" I ask him.

'"Yes", he says, all stern like, "if my conscience wasn't absolutely clear, I would, and grateful for the chance."

'"There's nothing wrong with my conscience", I tell him. "I can sleep as easy as yourself, sir, no offence intended", says I.

'"This is the second time in a week that your name has been bandied about", he tells me. I sat there, said nothing. "Will you not reconsider your decision about retirement, before a third piece of nastiness comes to light?"

'Well, gents, I'm afraid that did it. I'd sat quiet under the rest of his nonsense, but I wasn't standing for that, and I turned round and told him as much to his face.

'"In that case", says he, "you're suspended from duty, pending a summons to appear before a disciplinary tribunal. Hand over your warrant card!" says he, and that was that.' And Lestrade broke off, and helped himself to brandy.

There was a long silence, which neither Holmes nor I ventured to break. Eventually, Lestrade began again. 'Trouble is,' said he, 'for all my brave words I haven't the ghost of a chance of excusing my conduct. You see now what I meant, sir?' he asked Holmes.

There was another long silence. At last Holmes asked, 'You were, as I understand it, the junior officer on the case?'

Lestrade nodded. 'I know what you're thinking, Mr Holmes, that I was doing nothing more than just obeying the orders of a superior. But Superintendent Buller's dead, like I said, and Inspector White, well, I don't rightly know where he is these days. He had a seizure of some sort, and that left him pretty well crippled. He was living with his daughter's family over Hoxton way, last I heard. I meant to keep in touch, but you know how it is.'

'Indeed,' said Holmes. 'So, this Clayton has no other object upon which to vent his spleen, his quite understandable spleen, given the circumstances, than the unfortunate Inspector Lestrade?'

The unfortunate Inspector Lestrade nodded unhappily.

Holmes sat in silence for another long time, then said, choosing his words carefully, 'I fear that I cannot hold out any great hope for you, Lestrade.'

'I knew as much!'

'But, Holmes ...' I began, only to be silenced by an angry gesture.

'There are two distinct difficulties,' Holmes went on. 'Firstly, the improbability of finding any new evidence after ... what ... twenty years? Had I been in London, and in practice, of course, things might have been otherwise. But I was not. Secondly, and perhaps more to the point, what good would new evidence be? The man has been tried and the verdict given; now that verdict is set aside, and he is pronounced innocent. But he has still been tried, and under our laws he cannot be prosecuted again for the same offence.'

'Stay, though,' I broke in. 'Were they accused of only the one murder, that of the boy whose body was found, or of the others as well?'

'Excellent, Watson!' said Holmes, staring eagerly at Lestrade.

Lestrade shook his head sadly. 'They were charged with all five murders, Doctor,' said he. 'At the time, it seemed fine, we were being ordered to do something, anything. And there was a lot of upset where the boys lived, the East End, you know

27

what they're like down there. Just as it was with those "Ripper" murders a few years back, only more so, with the victims being so young, and all,' and he lapsed into a gloomy silence.

Holmes too sank back in his chair. 'That would appear to have been the only hope, and a mighty slender hope at that, and even that is gone. I have said that I cannot help,' he told Lestrade, 'and I must repeat that statement, for it is true enough. I would not wish to excite any false hopes in you, for that would be quite wrong, cruel in fact, and I would accordingly advise you to prepare for the worst that might happen. But we, Watson here and I, can listen to your version of events, and perhaps put the occasional question to you, so that you might be better ready to face the tribunal when the time comes. It may be that the process will stir in your mind something that might be material, though frankly I doubt it. You have given us the bare outline of events, but will you now tell us some of the details?'

Lestrade nodded. 'That's fair enough,' said he. 'Ask away.'

'Well, to begin with, what sort of a man was this Jacobson?'

'He was a rum one,' answered Lestrade. 'Odd. That sounds strange, I know. Any man who'd do a thing like that must be odd, you'll say, and that's right enough. But he was what my old mum would have called "slow". Not an imbecile, or anything of that sort, but easily led, impressionable. You know the sort I mean, the kind who, as a lad, would hear someone say "To put a brick through the vicarage window, that would be something like fun", and he'd go off and do it, with no thought for the consequences, whilst those who'd encouraged him were well out of it. The oddness, oddity, I should say, of the man, that was what struck you first. But then that very oddness, that was part of it, sir, with Clayton, I mean. You see, I couldn't have imagined Jacobson dreaming up that sort of nastiness himself, but I could believe in him tagging along while someone else did it.'

'The someone else being this Clayton?' suggested Holmes.

Lestrade nodded. 'So I thought.'

'The thought brings you little comfort, though?' Holmes went on.

Lestrade looked embarrassed. 'It's this way, Mr Holmes. The lad we were sure of, the one whose body we found, he was the last but one, and the newspapers had carried the stories of the first three. Now, I can easily see Jacobson reading those reports, and thinking he'd go out and do the same.'

'Are you suggesting that such was the case?' asked Holmes. 'If so, that would seem to indicate that possibly you believe in Clayton's innocence?'

'No, sir, Clayton was guilty right enough,' said Lestrade obstinately. 'But it bothered me, or I should say, it bothers me. Now. And back then, twenty years ago, but later, when it was over. When I was involved in the case itself, when the investigation was at its height, I just never thought of it.'

'And later, when you did?'

'Well, the jury had decided he was guilty. It was hardly for me to argue with that.'

'Indeed, no. And what sort of man was, or is, this Clayton?'

'He was odd, too, but in a different way. Cocksure, full of himself. That's why he stayed silent, I'm sure of that. As much as saying, "I know what I know, but I'm not telling you!"'

'He was of the same age as Jacobson?'

'Early twenties, yes,' said Lestrade.

'Which would make him in his middle forties now?' said I. 'He must be very resentful at having spent the best years of his life in prison.'

'You say he was "odd", Lestrade?' said Holmes with just a touch of impatience.

'Odd is the word, sir. He had no friends, apart from Jacobson, that is.'

'The two were friends? Not merely acquaintances?'

'We established that,' said Lestrade. 'They'd been seen talking together in the pub, that sort of thing. Not that we could ever connect that with the disappearances, but they were known to be friends.'

'But it seems to me,' said I, 'that if this Jacobson were of weak intellect, and being subject to some coercion … to put it no higher … he might simply have given you the first name that came into his head. If Clayton was his only friend, the only man he knew at all well, he might have clutched at his name.' I shook my head, for things looked worse by the minute.

Lestrade looked unhappy.

Holmes looked thoughtful. 'That is an excellent point,' said he. 'I interrupted you earlier, Lestrade; I was going to say that a conviction obtained solely on the basis of a confession by a third party seems very weak to me, and I can quite see why the death sentence was commuted. I am sure the appeal judges must have thought the same. And now Watson here provides one excellent reason for Jacobson's naming Clayton. Though of course there are others which will have occurred to you. It looks bad. Very bad! But continue, Lestrade.'

Looking even more unhappy than before, Lestrade went on, 'We searched Clayton's rooms, of course. There was nothing. Now, I don't just mean there was nothing that linked him to the crimes, though that's true enough. I mean rather that there was nothing at all of a personal nature. A few clothes, neatly hung in the closet, and nothing more. No letters, no photographs. And that was interesting, too.'

'How so?' asked Holmes.

'Well, first off, he had no wife, no lady friend. Wouldn't it be natural enough for him to have a few postcards from Paris, a lithograph or two of society beauties, something of that sort?'

'It is hardly a crime to be obsessively tidy,' I burst out, looking ruefully round our cluttered sitting room. 'Nor is it a crime not to possess pictures in dubious taste.'

'No, Doctor, but it's odd. That word again, you see,' said Lestrade. 'But my second point about photographs is just this. One of the few personal possessions we did find was a quarter-plate camera, with all the fixings, plates, chemicals, what have you. But the plates were all new, never … what do the photographers say? … never been exposed.'

'He may have bought the equipment recently,' said I.

'He hadn't. He'd bought it a couple of years before.'

'Well, perhaps he didn't like to spoil it by using it? Odd, I allow, but not unknown.'

'Again, no,' Lestrade told me. 'He'd bought the goods second-hand, from a chap who was getting married and needed the money.'

'And what did he have to say about it?' asked Holmes.

'Said he used to be keen, but hadn't done any photographing for some time.'

'It could be so?' I said.

'Oh, come, Doctor. If he had been so keen, why was there not a single print, a single negative plate, from the days when he was using the camera?'

'Well,' said Holmes, 'what was your theory?'

'Mine, Mr Holmes?' Lestrade looked startled. 'I had no theory. I just know that it was part of his oddness.'

'Again,' said I, 'odd though it may be, it is no crime to possess a camera which you don't use.'

Holmes shook his head. 'This is very insubstantial stuff, Lestrade. Were there other oddities to which you would draw our attention?' he asked.

'There was the relationship between Jacobson and Clayton,' said Lestrade. 'I have said that they were both loners, both solitary, each was the only friend the other had. Why should Jacobson, after holding out for so long under our questioning, then incriminate his only friend?'

'Doctor Watson had already supplied one possible explanation as to that,' said Holmes. 'Another might be that they were friends no longer, that there had been some falling-out, and that Jacobson sought to incriminate Clayton out of hatred, or spite, or jealousy, or whatever you choose to call it.'

'Agreed. But then why would he wait so long? Why not tell us right at the start?'

'He may perhaps have thought that if you had to ... well, to apply a little persuasion, let us say, it might sound more convincing than if he had blurted it out all at once?' suggested Holmes.

Lestrade shook his head. 'All very fine, Mr Holmes, all very logical, if you never met Jacobson. But I did meet him, and I can tell you that such a thing would never have occurred to him. A simple soul, like I say. Shallow. No guile, no deviousness in him.'

'What of motive, then?' I wanted to know. 'I can see men killing out of hate, or for money, or perhaps even for love, in the right, or wrong, circumstances. Was there any reason for the killings?'

Lestrade gave another shake of his head. 'No reason on this earth,' said he. 'There was no question of robbery, or anything of that sort. Sheer nastiness, Doctor, that's all the explanation I can give you, unsatisfactory though it is. Maybe Clayton had been beaten at school, and wanted to get his own back? Or maybe he'd been given the job of beating others, and acquired a taste for it? Or maybe he was just the sort of wretched little boy who enjoys pulling the wings off butterflies, and he never grew out of it?'

'You say "Clayton", as if you were sure of his guilt,' said Holmes.

'I am, sir, despite all the weighty evidence to the contrary.'

'And why? We come back to the same old question, Lestrade: what facts have you?'

'He was the sort,' said Lestrade. 'No women friends, indeed, no friends of any sort, apart from Jacobson.'

'Well,' I said, 'I must echo Holmes and say that this is pretty flimsy stuff, Lestrade. After all, he is not the only man to be indifferent to women,' I added, with a sidelong glance at Holmes.

'Well, then,' said Lestrade, with a touch of desperation, 'there was his behaviour when the verdict was announced. Jacobson and Clayton were standing side by side, of course, in the dock. And Jacobson looked at Clayton, and he spoke to him. Quietly, of course, but I was there next to him, almost, so I could hear him right enough, and he says, "I'm sorry, Algy, I didn't mean to tell them", and guess what Clayton said?' He paused. 'Nothing. Never said a word, not even, "Yes, and thanks very much, you little so-and-so!" Now, that would have been understandable, would it not, either way? Innocent or guilty, you might have expected him to be angry, or abusive, something, anything. But no. Not a sign of any emotion. He just looked at Jacobson, with no sign of anything in his eyes. Like a dead cod on a fishmonger's slab. And that's when I thought to myself, "Yes, you beggar. You're guilty all right!"'

'But you had not thought that before?' asked Holmes quickly.

Lestrade hesitated. 'I ... that is ... yes. Yes, sir, I was sure enough.'

'And yet you hesitated just now?'

'There were loose ends, sir, curious features of the case which were never resolved.'

'Ah.' Holmes sat up very straight and looked at Lestrade. 'It would be most interesting to hear of those.'

'The most telling one to me was the oddness of the two of them, Jacobson and Clayton, and I've just told you all about that. Then we found witnesses, of a sort, not any witnesses that we could take before a jury, but we found two men who'd seen something, or somebody. One had seen two men hanging about near where one of the boys was last seen and he gave us a description. Now, one of them might have been Clayton, but then by the same token he might have been anybody. But, and this is the interesting point, the other definitely wasn't Jacobson. Our "witness" was clear on that, for Jacobson was distinctive in appearance, his oddity extended even to that, and our man swore it couldn't possibly have been him. Well, these two men might have been two other men, like in the old music-hall joke. And they might have been there all proper and innocent.'

'And the second witness of sorts?'

'Three men ... not two, mark you, but three ... were seen loitering outside a little sweet shop, again near where one of the boys was last seen. No descriptions, that time, not that were any use.'

'You looked for these men?' asked Holmes.

'Insofar as was possible, but who, or what, were we looking for? With no proper description? Oh, we advertised, "Would three men, seen in So-and-so Street on such-and-such a date, please contact Scotland Yard", that sort of thing, but nothing came of it.'

'And Jacobson never referred to another, third, man?'

'Never. We asked him, but he just shrugged and mumbled the same old nonsense, that he deserved to hang.'

'If there were three men, and not two?' mused Holmes. 'But then ...' and he shook his head.

'Perhaps it was a home-grown version of the *omerta*, the oath of silence sworn by the *carbonari* and other secret societies?' I ventured. The two of them did not look as sceptical as I had feared they might, so I elaborated, 'Perhaps this Jacobson did only implicate Clayton by accident, as it were, when subjected to ... well, to violence. And neither of them implicated the third man, even when pressed.'

Lestrade shrugged, while Holmes merely looked at the ceiling. 'If these various other men were innocent, why did they not come forward?' he mused.

'Perhaps they did not read the newspapers,' said Lestrade. 'Or perhaps they simply did not recognize themselves in the advertisement? Or perhaps they were innocent of any involvement in the boys' disappearance, yet not entirely free from guilt in some other regard. They may perhaps have been "loitering with intent", as we say, in connection with some other crime?'

'H'mm.' I could see that Holmes was far from satisfied. 'As Watson so acutely observes, this is all very vague and insubstantial evidence. Jacobson is still in prison, I take it? The appeal court did not consider his case too?'

'Jacobson's dead,' said Lestrade. 'A couple of years ago, now. I didn't know myself, for you don't keep track of everyone you've put away, as you know, Mr Holmes, but the super mentioned it this morning.'

'H'mm. What became of the boys' families?'

Lestrade shrugged. 'A couple of them moved away, didn't want to stay and be reminded of what had happened. A couple did stay, just got on with things as best they could. Oh, and one caused a bit of a fuss, or tried to. A man called Tatton. Old soldier, he is, and he keeps going into his local, gets a skinful, and pulls out his old army bayonet ... "If ever they get out, I'll ..." do this, that and the other to them, I suppose. You know the kind of man I mean. A blowhard. A windbag. The local bobbies have taken him in once or twice for making a nuisance of himself, but the beaks treat him leniently, on account of what he went through.'

'Indeed.' Holmes leaned back in his chair, and regarded the ceiling again. 'I can only repeat my earlier remarks, Lestrade, and suggest that you prepare for the worst that may happen.' He sat up and gazed at the detective. 'Does the thought of that little pub really have not the slightest attraction?'

Lestrade managed a shaky laugh. 'I see I am in a minority when it comes to my retirement,' said he. He rose from his chair. 'I've taken up far too much of your time already, gents, so I'll be off. If ever I do get round to buying that pub, mind you, I'll expect to see you in there every evening.'

He shook hands with us. 'Shall I not go part of the way with you?' I asked him, fearing lest that he might come to some harm in his distressed condition, not to speak of the effects of the brandy so early in the day on one unused to it.

'No, thank you, Doctor,' he answered. 'I'll spring for a cab. I'd best be off home, tell the old lady the bad news. I can guess what she'll 'ave to say! Well, there's no help for it, she must be told.'

'You might just look up the address of this Inspector White, if he is still alive,' said Holmes casually.

Lestrade looked hard at him. 'You don't think there's anything to be made of that, sir?'

'I merely think that it might be as well to ask him if he has any recollection of the matter, that is all,' said Holmes. 'Talking to him may jog your own memory.'

'And feel free to call in here, talk to us at any time,' I told Lestrade. 'The very worst thing you could do is brood upon the matter in solitude.'

'I will, thank you, Doctor.'

'But I repeat my injunction not to raise your hopes, for I can see no satisfactory end to this business,' Holmes warned him.

'You are right, sir, unfortunately.' And on that dismal note, and without more ado, Lestrade left us.

For a long time, we sat in silence, then Holmes sighed. 'A bad business indeed, Watson.'

'You really see no hope for the poor devil?'

He shook his head. 'It is the old difficulty,' said he. 'Bricks without clay.' A bitter note crept into his voice. 'The investigation certainly seems to have been bungled in a spectacularly inept fashion, even by the undemanding standards of the official forces! Of course, in those early days things were handled a good deal more casually than would be acceptable now.'

'Yes, indeed. Lestrade himself seems to recognize that fact. Why, it almost seemed as if he were trying to prove this Clayton's innocence.'

'Perhaps he is trying to prove it to himself?'

'Guilty conscience, you mean?'

Holmes nodded.

'But why on earth did he not bring these points, all perfectly valid points, out when he was investigating the case?'

'Ah,' said Holmes, 'why indeed? He was the youngest member of the team, of course.'

'He did not want to flatly contradict the opinion of his superiors, you mean?'

'Well, it would do an ambitious man's career no good to do that, would it?' Holmes shook his head. 'For all that, I am less than happy with Lestrade's tale. Although I have had occasion to point out certain irregularities in his handling of the various cases in which we have both been involved, when it comes to ordinary routine police work he is nobody's fool. Why, then, as you say, did he miss these very obvious points? And so many of them. He saw them clearly enough later. There is something he is not telling us, I am sure of that. But what?'

'And why? He desperately needs your help, Holmes, that much is clear.'

Holmes leapt angrily to his feet, and strode to the window. 'What the devil am I expected to do, Watson? Look for three men, descriptions unknown, who were perhaps seen somewhere near a sweet shop twenty years ago? Who might very well have had nothing whatsoever to do with the case?'

'Well, if nothing else, at any rate you did what you said. You helped Lestrade collect his thoughts, ahead of his ordeal in the disciplinary hearing.'

He shook his head with some irritation. 'Watson, Watson! I had, of course, hoped for more than that. I had hoped that he might remember something, anything, which he might use on his own behalf.'

'Little point to that, surely? As we have said, the man cannot be tried a second time.'

'Perhaps not. But if Lestrade could bring forward some new evidence, if he could say in effect, "The appeal courts have reached their verdict, but these are the true facts", then it might save him some considerable trouble at his hearing. And it might save him from financial ruin in the civil courts, if this fellow Clayton does take civil proceedings against him, as he threatens.' He glanced at the clock. 'I have some errands to run, Doctor. I beg that you will excuse me.' And he was at the door and looking for coat and hat before he had finished speaking.

I sat alone when he had gone, brooding upon Lestrade's ugly little tale. I have seen great evil before, but ... thank Heaven ... nothing such as Lestrade had described. And then, too, I brooded upon the fate that might lie ahead of a man whom I had come to respect, and indeed to like. But to no good effect; if Holmes could see no hope for the unfortunate Inspector Lestrade, then for the life of me I could not.

Three

Over the next two or three days Lestrade took advantage of the invitation which we had so casually extended, and called in at 221B on several occasions. By now, Holmes had evidently found a case which did not need my attention, for he was absent much of the time on various mysterious errands. But I myself was still at something of a loose end, and Lestrade was in the same boat, and consequently the two of us spent some considerable time in talking, smoking and drinking rather more than was good for us.

Holmes, as I say, seemed entirely occupied with his own affairs, and I was thus considerably surprised when, at breakfast some four days after Lestrade had first broken his disturbing news, Holmes looked across at me and said, 'If you have nothing better to do today, Doctor, you might care to accompany me and have a word with this fellow Clayton.'

'I have certainly nothing that would keep from so interesting a meeting,' said I, 'but how on earth have you managed to arrange it?'

'Oh, it was simple enough. I merely left my card, with a message to say that I should be grateful for a few moments of his time.'

'Well,' said I, laughing, 'that is indeed simple enough!'

'And this morning he has sent me a note to say that he will see me today, at half past ten. I should be happy if you could come with me.'

'He is doubtless intrigued to know what Mr Sherlock Holmes might want with him?'

'Doubtless.'

'Although he must realize that you are, so to speak, on the same side as Lestrade, and therefore unlikely to be sympathetic to his ... to Clayton's, that is ... cause?'

'That is true to some extent,' said Holmes thoughtfully. 'And yet the superficial reader of your accounts might perhaps form the impression that Lestrade and his colleagues are sometimes at loggerheads with me. Indeed, some of your tales actually go so far as to suggest that I am occasionally on the side of the criminal.'

'Never!'

'Well, what about that business of the blue carbuncle? My dear fellow, the Countess of Morcar was positively angry with me for letting the thief go free.'

'But she got her jewel back, Holmes,' said I, puzzled.

'Ah, yes, but then she wanted her revenge on the man who had stolen it. The rich can be so damnably vindictive. And I will not burden you with what Lestrade had to say on the matter! I come increasingly to the opinion that I must forbid you to publish any more of my cases, until I shall have retired from active practice. Indeed, I fancy I have had occasion to mention this once or twice before.'

'We can discuss that later, Holmes!' said I hastily.

'Indeed.' He stood up. 'And now, if you are quite ready, Doctor?'

I followed him outside. Holmes hailed a cab, and gave the driver an address in the vicinity of Grosvenor Square.

'I had not realized this fellow Clayton had such fashionable lodgings,' said I in some surprise.

'The house is not his, though. He is staying with friends at the moment.'

'I thought he had none? Did Lestrade not describe him as a solitary individual?'

'Ah, but that was before his trial, conviction, virtual retrial and subsequent release,' said Holmes. 'He is now an object of interest, the pathetic victim of a corrupt and wicked legal system.' There was a curious note, which I could not quite place, in his voice.

'You sound almost as if you believe that,' I told him.

Holmes shrugged, and there was a reluctance about his answer. 'Well, there is at least a possibility that he is innocent, is there not? The fact that he is, or perhaps I should say that his new friends are, making much of recent events does not necessarily mean that he is not an innocent victim, et cetera. No, Watson, I am going to this interview with an open mind, not so much to try to find something which will help Lestrade as to find out, if it be possible, the truth of the matter.'

'And if it transpires that Lestrade was wholly culpable?'

Holmes looked out of the window in silence, as if he had not heard me, for some considerable time, before saying, 'Damnation, Watson!'

'Really, Holmes!'

He laughed. 'I am sorry, Doctor, but it is deuced awkward, you must agree. Despite our little differences, I actually like Lestrade. Why the devil did he not insist on making his doubts known in the first place? And then, having kept silent at the time, for whatever reason, why did he not discuss the matter with his superiors later, or come along and talk it over with you and me? If nothing else, Lestrade is guilty of a gross error of judgement. If there is more, if the worst comes to the worst ...' and he stopped again.

'Well?'

'Well, I shall stand by him, as I am sure will you. So far as is possible, that is to say, by giving him what comfort and reassurance may be possible.'

'It seems little enough,' said I.

'If the worst does come to the worst, doubtless his friends will stand by him in a more tangible fashion,' said Holmes shortly, relapsing into a brooding silence.

I said nothing: I had myself had some small proofs of Holmes's generosity, although he would be very angry if I were to mention them. I knew well enough that he would not let Lestrade down if it came to it. And, moreover, I flattered myself that I too would not be found altogether wanting in that respect, despite the perpetually unpredictable nature of a writer's bank balance. Somehow, Holmes and I would see Lestrade through.

The cab came to a halt before a large and impressive house. 'There's money here,' said I.

'Indeed,' said Holmes, a gloomy note in his voice.

'And?' I asked.

'It will not make our task any easier, Watson. It is always more difficult to deal with the rich.' He shook his head, as if to dispel grim thoughts. I rang the bell, and the door was opened by a solemn butler, who gravely took our cards and invited us to wait in a side room. After a short wait, we were shown into a large drawing room, furnished in a modern, but I must say a most elegant, style.

There was a considerable crowd in the room, both men and women; but I have to record that the occupants were by no means as elegant as the room itself. I trust I am not more censorious of my fellow human beings than the next man. Indeed, the rough and tumble of my life has tended to make me somewhat uncritical in that regard. But for all that, I cannot say with any truth that any of that throng impressed me at all favourably. Mostly they were young, between twenty and thirty years of age, and all pretty obviously well to do. For the most part, the men were languid creatures, with the dull complexions that speak of too much time spent indoors, and they were dressed so very fashionably that it was almost affectation. I can only say that had they been put up for membership of my club ... which is very far from the most exclusive in London ... the number of white marbles would have been low. If anything, the women were worse; every bit as unhealthy looking as their menfolk, with hair cropped shorter than appeals to my own taste, they seemed to me to have chosen their costumes at some rummage sale. Indeed, by comparison, the men looked positively gorgeous ... until you looked at their faces, which managed to look both smug and dissatisfied. In the course of a long and often trying life I have never encountered a more uninviting assembly.

I became aware that I was being introduced to the man we had come to see, Algernon Clayton. He was perhaps the most unprepossessing of the whole assembly, well under the middle height, with the same pasty face as the rest of them. I reluctantly shook his hand, and noted that he avoided meeting my gaze, and spoke out of the corner of his mouth. I remembered that he just been released from prison, and tried to make all the allowances I could, but I must say that I was not very favourably impressed by him.

'You are here, I take it, as representatives of Lestrade?' said he, a sneer in his voice which he did not take the trouble to conceal. 'Can he not afford a proper lawyer, then?'

There was a sort of appreciative snigger from the rest of them at this. Holmes, in the calmest possible manner, replied, 'We are here on our own behalf only, I assure you. Although I will not deny that Inspector ...' and he stressed the word ... 'Inspector Lestrade is a personal friend of Watson and myself. We would naturally wish to do what we might for him in his hour of need, if we can.'

The last phrase was evidently not lost upon Clayton. 'You may well find that there is nothing you can do for him,' said he.

'We shall see,' said Holmes.

Holmes's calm demeanour clearly impressed Clayton, though he strove to conceal this fact. 'Do you want to ask me something?' said he, a touch hesitantly.

'I scarcely think there is very much use our rehashing old questions,' said Holmes. 'What is more to the point is what action do you now propose to take?'

'Ohoh!' cried Clayton to the assembled multitude, 'he wants to know what we're going to do to his little friend.' Quickly recovering his composure, he thrust his face a few inches from Holmes's in a most offensive fashion, and said, 'Twenty years! That's what I spent inside, twenty stinking years. I want some recompense for that. Money, first ... do you know what those beggars have offered me as what they call an *ex gratia* payment in compensation?'

I paraphrase his speech slightly; he did not say 'beggars' but something close to it, and it pains me to record that the women in the room, so far from showing any signs of consternation, actually laughed as he spoke. If I were in Holmes's place, I fear that Clayton would have felt the toe of my boot. The fact that Holmes did not turn a hair speaks volumes for my friend's forbearance and powers of self-control. 'I cannot imagine,' said he. 'What was it, then?'

Clayton looked slightly abashed, and stood back a little. 'Fifty guineas,' said he. 'Fifty blinking guineas! Does that strike you as equitable?'

Holmes said nothing. Clayton looked at me. 'How does it strike you, Doctor?'

'It depends upon whether you were guilty,' said I. 'If you were not, sir, then frankly it seems to me to be paltry in the extreme. But then governments have never been exactly noted for their over-generosity.'

There was a scattered round of applause at this, and one of the men stood up and shook my hand. 'Well said, Doctor,' he told me. 'As to Algy's guilt or innocence, that has already been established by the appeal court. But you are right to say that fifty guineas is paltry. Typical of the arrogance of a rotten system. Why, Bertie, there … ' and he indicated a particularly repulsive specimen lounging on a *chaise longue* in the manner of one of the more depraved Roman emperors, with a vacant-faced woman gazing adoringly at him from either side … 'Bertie's father is the proprietor of a newspaper,' and he mentioned the name of a scandal-mongering rag, 'and Bertie's going to write a piece about the whole sorry business. The true story of Algy's twenty year ordeal. And the paper will pay Algy a hundred and fifty sovs for it.'

I reflected sourly that Bertie, for all that he might well dislike 'a rotten system,' was not averse to using his father's money or his father's reputation. But, with a supreme effort of will, I followed Holmes's splendid example and said nothing.

'But that's not enough, not by a long chalk,' added Clayton. 'I've worked it all out for you,' and he produced a little notebook. 'Twenty years, and I might have earned two hundred a year. That's fair, isn't it? Why, an ordinary stock-broker's clerk would get as much. That alone comes to four thousand. And that represents no more than the money I might have earned. There will also have to be some reckoning, some recompense for the loss of my freedom, what should have been the best years of my life, the injustice and injury I have suffered!' His colourless face became almost animated, and his voice rose until it was almost a scream, as he recited this litany. He subsided somewhat, and ended prosaically, 'The final figure I have is ten thousand pounds.'

Holmes, as composed as ever, replied, 'Between fifty guineas and ten thousand pounds there is a great gulf fixed. Think you honestly that the authorities will concur with your computation?'

'It isn't the authorities ... as you call 'em ... that I plan to sue,' hissed Clayton. 'It's that so-and-so Lestrade!'

'No need for blackguardly language, sir,' I told him. 'I might possibly find some sympathy within me for your predicament, but you will discover that it serves your cause better to keep a civil tongue in your head.'

The young man who had spoken earlier said hastily, 'You must excuse Algy, gentlemen, for he is somewhat overwrought, and understandably so. But it is not entirely a question of money, for what, after all, is that but mere dross? No, it is rather a question of ... of ...' he floundered slightly.

'Revenge?' suggested Holmes.

'Well, sir, if you will have the plain word for the plain sentiment. And why not, pray? After all, Algy has much to be bitter about.'

'Bitter?' said Clayton, with a mirthless laugh. 'I should think I was! Those three somethings ruined my life, when all is said and done.'

'I am sure that they acted in good faith,' said Holmes.

Clayton seemed unable to speak in response to this, but the young man who appeared to be Clayton's spokesman said, 'Algy does not see it in that light, Mr Holmes, and nor do his friends here,' and he waved a hand to indicate the others. 'It seems to us that there was some strong personal animosity towards Algy, and that we cannot have. Of the three men who conducted, if that is the right word, the police inquiry, one is dead, and one is, as I understand it, not in full possession of his faculties. That leaves only this fellow Lestrade.'

'And it is from Lestrade that you propose to seek redress?' said Holmes.

'Too something true!' sneered Clayton.

'I have already asked you, sir,' said I, 'to moderate your language before these ladies.' This was greeted with a sort of snicker of amusement ... or perhaps it was contempt ... from those ladies of whom I spoke. I could not restrain myself from adding, 'Although on reflection perhaps my powers of observation are as flawed as your speech!'

This was not entirely well received by the assembled harpies. Holmes cut in hastily, 'You must realize, sir, that Inspector Lestrade is far from a rich man. It would be unrealistic to expect him to find he sum you mentioned.'

'That's his concern,' said Clayton. 'I'll settle for whatever he has.'

'He will be ruined,' said Holmes. 'Always assuming that your action is successful.'

'Ruined?' said Clayton. 'And why shouldn't he be ruined? Didn't he ruin my life, the so-and-so?'

The young man added, 'As to the action being successful, I hardly think that a jury will disagree with the appeal court ruling.'

'You would not consider a lesser, a more realistic, sum in exchange for dropping this hounding of Lestrade?' asked Holmes.

There was a roar of laughter at this, and remarks like, 'We have them on the run now!' from the motley throng.

Holmes stood up. 'I see that there is nothing further to discuss,' said he. 'We shall accordingly take our leave of you.'

And leave we did, with our tails pretty well between our legs. They did not exactly jeer as we walked out of the room with what shreds of dignity we could muster, but I felt that it was a close-run thing.

As we stood on the pavement looking for a cab, Holmes shook himself, as if to remove the dust of the place from his garments. He glanced at me, laughed in his peculiar noiseless fashion, and said, 'I have had some painful interviews in the course of my professional career, but that was perhaps one of the least pleasurable. What say you, friend Watson?'

'A poisonous crew, Holmes, that's what I say! They certainly have it in for poor Lestrade.'

'They do indeed. What of Clayton? How did he impress you?'

'A foul-mouthed cur, Holmes. I cannot say I would have been favourably impressed by his language or appearance were I on any jury that tried him.'

'Oh, you may be sure that his friends will coach him until he is word perfect before it comes to court. Indeed, you have probably done him a very considerable service, letting him know just what sort of behaviour does or does not please a solid British juryman.'

'Sorry I spoke, now!'

Holmes laid a hand on my sleeve. 'My dear fellow, I would not have it any other way. You did what you thought was right, and damn the consequences. But, apart from his language and behaviour, did you feel that he was honest?'

'Hard to say. Making allowances for his outlook ... well, I suppose his antagonism towards Lestrade was certainly honest enough, Holmes.'

'I agree with you there. And that other fellow was right enough when he said that a judge and jury must attach a good deal of weight to the verdict of the appeal court. That was why I tried to chaffer with them, to come to some accommodation, but it was a waste of time, as you saw. They are indeed set upon their pound of flesh.'

'I am bound to say, Holmes, that it looks bad. Ignoring Clayton's filthy Billingsgate speech, he does seem to be convinced that he has a case. And so do those others, even if they are unprepossessing. If he has convinced them, he might well convince others. I am bound to say that I was not altogether unmoved by his evident sincerity, although it could have been better expressed.'

'That is quite true. And with a decent lawyer, a sympathetic judge and jury, the matter might not go entirely in Lestrade's favour.' As we settled down in the cab, he repeated thoughtfully, 'Yes, you are quite right in saying that they plan to ruin Lestrade. I wonder ...' and he lapsed into a brooding silence.

I have frequently seen Holmes at something of a loss when he is on a case, but in those instances there has always been some glimmer of hope, however faint, that he would find the trail again. With this sorry business, though, what could he do? It was all so long ago, and had been so very confused even when it was fresh and new. It was in a silence as deep as Holmes's own, and with a very heavy heart, that I sat in that cab as we returned to Baker Street.

The page boy opened the door for us. 'Any callers, Billy?' asked Holmes.

'Inspector Lestrade, sir. He's up in your sitting room now.'

Four

'I should say nothing of our interview with Clayton for the moment,' advised Holmes as we went upstairs.

'Very well.' Feeling that I was at last truly being taken into Holmes's confidence by being thus encouraged to use his own trick of revealing as little information as possible, I opened the door, and went into our sitting room. Lestrade made as if to rise as I entered, but I waved him back to his chair.

'Any more news, Lestrade?' I asked, as I hung up my coat and hat.

'Not unless you count an argument – that is, a discussion, with the wife.'

'Ah.'

'It's this retirement business, Doctor,' said Lestrade, becoming talkative as Holmes and I sat down opposite him. 'Now, the wife is usually the most pleasant and good-natured of women, but she has got it into her head that I should do what the superintendent suggested, and take my pension. "You're not getting any younger", she tells me. As if I didn't know that all too well! And, "You've talked often enough about what you'll do when you retire", and "If they say you were incompetent, you might be dismissed with no pension at all." All quite true of course,' and he shrugged.

'But it smacks of running away?'

Lestrade nodded. 'It does that. And more than that, for if I take my pension and leave the force, I'm as good as admitting my guilt, saying I know that I was wrong.'

I started to speak, changed my mind, and coughed to hide my confusion.

'Spit it out, Doctor,' advised Lestrade. 'It might be a gold watch.'

'Very well, then. Look here, Lestrade, you and I have known each other a good long time now, and we can, I believe, be honest with each other. You must see how this matter looks to a dispassionate observer: a conviction obtained solely on the basis of a confession, not by the accused man, but by someone else, a third party, as it were? It is a very shaky foundation upon which to build a prosecution.'

'Maybe it seems that way to you, Doctor,' began Lestrade in a stubborn fashion, 'but ...' and he broke off as Holmes raised an eyebrow. 'Well, Mr Holmes? You see that Doctor Watson here is insistent that I take my pension and make the best of it. How say you?' he asked with a curious embarrassed sort of laugh.

'It matters little what I think, or indeed what anyone else thinks. I gather that you are still not of that mind?'

'I'm not, Mr Holmes,' said Lestrade firmly.

Holmes was about to speak when there came a ring at the street door, followed by footsteps on our stair. I recognized the brisk step of the pageboy, but not the rather ponderous tread of the visitor who followed him. Billy tapped on our door, opened it, and announced, 'Mr Jabez Wilson, to see Mr 'Olmes.'

'Good Lord!' said I.

Lestrade raised an eyebrow as Mr Wilson, the same rather portly, red-headed pawnbroker whom I had last seen perhaps five or six years previously, entered the room, and gazed at us with his sunken little eyes.

'Well, this is an entirely unexpected pleasure, Mr Jabez Wilson,' said Holmes, shaking our visitor's pudgy hand. 'But you do not tell me that you have become enmeshed in another little affair such as that of the Red-headed League, I trust?' he added, a twinkle in his eye.

Our visitor chuckled. 'No, Mr Holmes! One puzzle of that sort is enough for me. But I can see I've got you stumped, sir, which is a rare event with you.'

'I own you have,' said Holmes. He turned to the Scotland Yard man. 'You will have heard about the little matter of the French gold, a few years back, Lestrade?'

'I have, Mr Holmes. Of course, I wasn't involved, worse luck. It made the reputation of Peter Jones, who was,' added Lestrade, a touch of envy apparent in his voice.

'Indeed. But we are interrupting you, Mr Wilson. You have, as you say, intrigued us all.'

'Well, I haven't forgotten that business, Mr Holmes, nor how you helped me out with clearing it up, and so when the lad came to my little shop and said you were asking about jewellery, I paid particular attention. And this time, sir, I think I may be the one to help *you* solve your problem.'

Lestrade looked puzzled by all this, and I probably did the same, for I had no notion as to what was going on. Holmes told us, 'I sent the irregular forces out to scour the jewellers and pawnshops, with a description of the jewellery taken in the robbery at Sir Octavius' town house.' He asked Wilson, 'You have seen some of the items, then?'

Wilson looked doubtful. 'Not recently, Mr Holmes.' He took a grimy and crumpled piece of paper from his pocket, and smoothed it out. 'This is your list, sir.' He indicated a line with a thick finger, and read, '"White gold necklace, with thirty-seven diamonds, old cut". That's the item, Mr Holmes. Only ...'

'Yes?'

'It wasn't recent, you see, sir. It was more like a year ago that I bought something similar.'

'Ah.' Holmes took from his pocket a picture which had clearly been clipped from the society pages of some popular journal. 'Was this the man who pawned the necklace?'

Wilson shook his head without bothering to look at the portrait. 'It wasn't a man at all, sir. It was a woman, I'm sure of that.'

'Do you have it still? Or was the pledge redeemed, and if so, by whom?'

'Again, sir, it wasn't left as security for a loan, it was an outright sale.'

'I see. Is that not a little unusual?'

51

Wilson nodded. 'It is, Mr Holmes. But then the lady was insistent, and the price asked was so reasonable ... you understand? I'm afraid it went, sir, I sold it the week after, so I can't show it you. It may not be what you wanted after all?' he added anxiously.

'It does not sound as if it were,' said Holmes. He took a half sovereign from his pocket, adding, 'But this is for your trouble.'

Wilson left, after thanking Holmes profusely.

'I took the descriptions of the missing items from the newspaper reports,' said Holmes when the door had closed after our visitor. 'I did not expect any outcome from my enquiries, but it would have been remiss of me to neglect the obvious.'

'We made our own enquiries, but with no result,' said Lestrade, with some annoyance.

'Ah, but you were asking about recent sales,' said Holmes. 'And besides, these fellows often find it easier to talk to me than to the official forces. No reflection on you, my dear Lestrade, but it is a fact. Had Mr Jabez Wilson not been an old acquaintance, I doubt if he would have come here today.'

'I don't see as it takes us very far anyway,' said Lestrade, somewhat mollified. 'If the piece was sold a year ago, and the murder and robbery were just recent ...'

'Ah, but consider this if you will, as a speculative possibility only. Sir Octavius had been taking his wife's jewellery for some time, piece by piece, pawning or selling it to pay his immediate debts, and perhaps telling his wife some tale of having it cleaned, or the like. When her suspicions reached the danger point, he resolved his problem by direct means. How say you to that?'

'By the lord Harry, yes!' said Lestrade, a look of triumph on his face. 'You have it, Mr Holmes, that's the explanation, no doubt of that.' He sank back, his face falling. 'But how to bring it home to him? That's the difficulty. He would never pawn the stuff himself, or sell it, he'd use some agent, as in this instance. Even if we could identify the pieces, Sir Octavius would be in the clear. He would be sure to say he knew nothing, that his wife had sold the pieces, or maybe that he had done so with her knowledge and full consent. After all, the poor woman isn't here to contradict anything he may choose to say, is she?'

'There would be some awkward questions, though?' said I. 'After all, he had told you that these things had been stolen recently.'

Lestrade shook his head. 'He would just say that his wife had sold them without his knowledge, like I say, and that he genuinely thought they had been stolen. Or perhaps that he knew but lied to protect his poor wife's reputation, that she drank, or was being blackmailed, and needed the cash for that. He's capable of anything, I tell you. No, Doctor, we're sunk. Unless we can shake his alibi, and I don't hold out much hope there.'

'The alibi, to be sure,' mused Holmes. He thought a moment, then went on, 'Perhaps not. But we have one crack in the seemingly impregnable edifice, so who can say that others may not appear in due course?'

'You may be right,' said Lestrade without any conviction. He consulted his watch. 'I've taken up too much of your time already, sir, so I'll be off. By the by, I did as you asked me, and enquired about old Inspector White. I have his address here.'

'Indeed?' Holmes stood up. 'Have you plans for the remains of the day, at all?'

Lestrade shook his head.

'Watson? Are you engaged this afternoon?'

'Not I. Did you propose to visit this Inspector White?'

'He may be able to tell us something,' said Holmes, 'although I think it improbable. Still, it is better than sitting here feeling sorry for ourselves,' and he gave us a lead by recovering the coat and hat he had just hung up.

Within a very short time we were all sitting in a cab, bound for Shoreditch, where Lestrade told us Inspector White's family lived.

'Your Algernon Clayton is certainly not a sympathetic character,' said Holmes as we rattled along.

'What, have you seen him, then?' asked Lestrade.

'Yes,' said Holmes. 'Watson and I spoke to him this very morning.'

'Oh? And what has he to say for himself, then?'

'Much as you might imagine. He has gathered quite a crowd about him.'

'Who are they?' asked Lestrade.

'Oh, mostly young people of radical, or would-be radical, disposition. I gather they have rallied to his cause,' answered Holmes. 'Not too surprising, because every enthusiast for the *fin de siècle*, everyone who seeks the label "decadent" for themselves, naturally sees the established order, the government, the forces of law and order, as legitimate objects of their scorn.'

'That's him all over! I beg your pardon, Mr Holmes,' said Lestrade, 'I should not have interrupted you, and I'd like to know what passed between you.'

'Remarkably little,' said Holmes, with an inclination of the head to show that he understood Lestrade's impatience. 'He has, it emerged, sold what one of his associates called something like "the true story of his twenty year ordeal" to one of the more sensational Sunday newspapers, for an undisclosed sum.'

Lestrade groaned. 'And once them fellows get their claws into me, I'm done, good and proper. You know as well as I do, that they're only concerned with selling their rags, and don't care how they do it, or who they ruin in the process.'

Holmes went on, 'Clayton did confirm that he is looking at the possibility of bringing a civil action against you, Lestrade. He has calculated it all out, "twenty years", said he, "at two hundred a year, that's four thousand pounds" ...'

'Four thousand!' cried Lestrade.

'And even that, according to him, was merely the money he might have earned were he a free man. "There must also be a reckoning", he went on, "of the loss of my freedom, and the injustice and injury done to me", and the final sum he mentioned was ten thousand.'

Lestrade sank back, aghast. 'Ten! Ten thousand! Well, the sole consolation is that he might as well say a million, and have done. For I've no more chance of paying the one than the other. Mr Holmes, ten thousand pounds! My little bit of savings don't amount to more than a few hundred. And if that goes, we'll be ruined, the wife and me. Ruined. Well, I don't know, and that's a fact,' and he passed a hand over his brow.

Holmes laid a hand on Lestrade's sleeve. 'Do not be too despondent,' said he. 'It may not be as bad as all that.'

'Did Clayton say anything that might give you hope, then?' I asked at once. 'For, to be honest …' and I broke off.

Holmes did not answer me directly. 'He is certainly very bitter about Lestrade here,' he said. 'That must have struck you, Watson?'

'Indeed. It was palpable.'

'And genuine?' asked Lestrade, with a sneer.

'It struck me that way,' said I. 'I am sorry to be so blunt, Lestrade, but so it seemed to me.'

'His hatred of Lestrade was genuine enough, I'll swear to that,' said Holmes thoughtfully. 'As for the rest … well, frankly I heard nothing that would lead me to feel any great optimism.' And he sank back in his seat just as Lestrade had done, and drummed with his fingers upon the window. I had a very gloomy pair of travelling companions for the remainder of the journey.

The cab turned into a narrow and rather dirty street, and drew up before a house that looked no different from its neighbours. Lestrade looked up at the windows, then at the door, then consulted a scrap of paper. 'This is the place,' he concluded, and knocked at the door, which was shabby but clean.

'Shabby but clean' also describes the woman who opened the door in answer to Lestrade's knock. She was perhaps forty years old, and her face bore the marks of a life that had been far from easy. She looked apprehensively from one to another of us.

'Mrs White?' asked Lestrade.

'No, sir. My name's Williams.'

'It was an Inspector White we sought.'

'Ah, that's dad. My father, that is. You'll be friends of his?' she asked anxiously.

55

'Is he at home? Could you tell him Inspector Lestrade is here?'

'Won't you come in?' She stood aside, to allow us to enter the house, which was cramped but spotlessly clean. 'I'll just tell him you're here,' and Mrs Williams disappeared into an inner room.

We heard her say something in a low tone, then another voice, thin and querulous, the voice of an old man, called out, 'Show them in, girl!'

Mrs Williams reappeared, and ushered us into a tiny parlour, where a very old man, shrunken and wizened, sat in a wheelchair. A couple of small children regarded us with enormous eyes, but Mrs Williams, with a certain amount of tugging at collars, and one or two judicious cuffings of ears, cleared them out of the room. She turned at the door, and said, 'If you'd like a cup of tea, please let me know,' and then she closed the door after her.

'Sit down,' said the old man, 'you make the place look untidy,' and he waved us to ordinary wooden chairs. 'Not what you're used to, maybe,' he added, 'but it's all there is.'

'It's well enough,' said Lestrade shortly. 'Now, then, do you know me?'

'Know you? Of course, I know you. Didn't my daughter tell me who you were? Not that I needed telling,' he added with a cackle, 'I'd have known you anywhere.' He held out a claw-like hand to Lestrade. 'I expected to see you,' he went on, nodding to a newspaper which lay on the scrubbed deal table. 'And it's good to see you, even though it took a calamity to bring you here.'

'Ah, well,' said Lestrade, embarrassed. 'I always meant to come, but ... well, you know how it is, Chalky ... Inspector White, I mean.'

'Chalky will do,' said the old man. 'Do you think I didn't know you called me that, behind my back? And who are these two?' he asked.

'This is Mr Sherlock Holmes, and this is Doctor Watson.'

'Sherlock Holmes?' The old man tried to whistle, with limited success. I recollected that he had had some kind of seizure or stroke, and concluded that it had affected his speech somewhat. 'Well, I've heard of you, sir, even out here. And Doctor Watson! Many a happy hour your stories have given me, sir. Far better than most of the rubbish in the *Strand* and such-like trash, even if they are a bit fantastic at times.'

'I assure you, sir, that I record merely the bald facts as they occurred.'

'I have lost count of the number of times I have accused you of embellishing your accounts, Watson,' Holmes told me, 'and now even your readers are coming round to my way of thinking. You are evidently an acute observer, sir,' he told Inspector White.

'Inspector White here ... Chalky, if he'll allow the impertinence from a youngster like me ... was the best copper on the force in his day,' said Lestrade.

'I was, too,' added the old man.

'I am sure that you were,' said Holmes, 'and it was in what I might term a professional capacity that we wished to see you. You say that you have read of the release of Algernon Clayton?' and he nodded towards the newspaper on the table.

'That I have, Mr Holmes.'

'And was he guilty, think you?'

'Guilty? He was a rum 'un, right enough. Guilty? Aye, he was guilty. Guilty as Judas Iscariot! And why the beggars have let him off, I couldn't begin to tell you.'

'And why do you say that?' asked Holmes. 'Was there anything significant which did not emerge at the trial?'

The old man thought a moment. 'No, sir, I can't say as there was,' he said at last.

'But it seems to me from what Lestrade has said, that there was some doubt as to the case against Clayton?' said Holmes.

'Not in my mind, sir. I was sure enough that he was guilty,' said Inspector White stubbornly.

'The appeal court thought otherwise, though?'

The old man shrugged his shoulders. 'Their opinion, isn't it? They have theirs, I got mine, and that's all there is to it. I was certain of Clayton's guilt, and my superintendent, Superintendent Buller, his name was, he went along with me. And Lestrade here.'

'But now Lestrade here seems to think that there were many loose ends to the investigation,' Holmes persisted.

The old man shrugged again. 'There's always loose ends, sir, to any detective work. You'll know that as well as anyone, Mr Holmes.'

'But there seem so very many in this instance?'

'It might look that way, now. At the time, we were satisfied enough.'

'I cannot think why I did not say anything at the time,' said Lestrade suddenly. 'There were, as Mr Holmes says, so many loose ends that I ought to have noticed them.'

'Ah, well.' The old man laughed until he choked, and I feared that my professional services might be required. 'I'm all right,' he told us, recovering himself somewhat. 'No, gents, I could tell you why Mr Lestrade here didn't notice those loose ends, as he calls 'em. Why don't you ask him?'

'Lestrade?' said Holmes, mystified.

Lestrade looked at the old man. 'I'm sure I've no idea what he's talking about, Mr Holmes. What was it then, Chalky?'

'You don't remember, then?'

'Remember what?'

'Her.'

'Her?' Lestrade clearly had no idea what the old man was talking about.

'Her. Bessie, was it?'

'Bessie?' Lestrade frowned. 'I still don't ... oh!' and he stopped, and flushed.

'Well, Lestrade?' said Holmes.

'Nothing, Mr Holmes, sir. Nothing, I assure you.'

The old man laughed immoderately again. 'He won't tell you!' said he, sounding for all the world like a naughty child. 'But I could. You ask him, gents. Make him tell you.' He laughed again, then grew serious as he looked at Lestrade. 'And this Clayton, now? Out to make trouble, is he?'

'That's the way of it,' said Lestrade.

The old man nodded. 'He always struck me as a vicious cur,' said he. 'Of course, with Buller being dead, and me not so far off, it'll be you he's after, will it?'

'It is,' said Lestrade.

'I thought as much. Well, if there's anything I can do, count on me. Not that I expect there will be,' said the old man cheerfully. 'And I reckon nobody else will be able to do much either ... or want to. They won't want any mud sticking to them, you see,' he explained to Holmes and me. 'Throw him to the blinking wolves, they will.'

On that cheerful note, we took our leave. On the way back, Holmes looked at Lestrade and asked, 'What did Mr White mean about this ... Bessie, was it?'

Lestrade looked embarrassed. 'It had nothing to do with the matter, Mr Holmes,' he said.

'Mr White seemed to think otherwise.'

'He's an old man, sir, he doesn't know what he's saying.'

'He seemed alert enough to me.' When Lestrade did not reply, Holmes went on, 'Come, Lestrade. You sought my assistance, remember, I did not come to you. If I am to do anything for you, then you must not hide anything from me.'

'That's true enough, sir.' Lestrade sat back and stared out of the window. 'It was twenty years back, and I'd all but forgotten it,' said he. 'That's true as well, though Chalky wouldn't believe me. I'd been married some three or four years, and the wife and me ... well, to be blunt, we'd had a devil of a row, and off she goes to her mother's. I was almost frantic, Mr Holmes, wondering if I'd get her back, blaming myself for what had happened. You'll know what I mean, I'm sure, Doctor Watson?'

'Indeed, yes! That is to say, I can readily imagine it,' said I.

'Well, I was on my own in the house, and I felt the need of someone to talk to.'

'A sympathetic ear, as it were?' said I.

'You have it, Doctor. Of course, if I'd known either of you gents back then, it'd have been your ears I'd have been bending. But as it was, I didn't know just who to talk to. And then I thought of Bessie. But that's all it was, I swear, just talk. Just someone to talk to.'

'And who exactly was Bessie?' asked Holmes.

'Bessie was ... well, Mr Holmes, she'd been no better than she ought to be, if you take my meaning. It's this way, sir. A few years before all this Clayton business first happened, when I was just a young copper on the beat, I was strolling along, waiting to go off duty, when under a street lamp I spies a young lady, plying her trade, as it were. Well, I went up to her, ready to run her in, and blow me if I didn't recognize her. It was this Bessie I'm telling you about, and I knew her from years before. Matter of fact, we'd been at school together. Now, it's a small world, isn't it, and all? Well, I gave her a piece of my mind all right, told her that by rights I should take her along to the station, but that I wouldn't, provided I didn't see her there again.'

'And?'

'And I didn't, Mr Holmes. She took my little speech to heart, and invested her bit of savings in a little eating place. Nothing so grand as a restaurant, or cafe, or anything of that sort, just a little workmen's eating place where you could get pie and mash, a cup of tea, that kind of thing. Kept it nice, and didn't take any cheek from the customers, neither, though some of 'em tried, for she was a good-looker. I got into the way of dropping in there myself from time to time, just for a cuppa and a natter. Handy for the Yard, it was, though I haven't been in there for years now. Anyway, when all this upset happened, I called in there, and talked to her, most nights. When I could get away, that is, for we were pretty busy, as you may imagine. But it was only talk, sir, I promise you! Not that I didn't sometimes think ... well, you know. Bessie, she was a good-looker, all right. But then the wife's mother, she came round to the house in a cab, and talked to me, said she'd got rid of Violet, that's the wife, of course, once, and didn't want her back there for the rest of her days, so we'd best sort it out quick. A bit rough, the wife's mother, but a heart of gold. Anyway, we sorted it out, and we've never had a cross word since. Or not until this latest matter of my retirement, and even then we haven't what you'd call argued, not as such.'

'And what became of Bessie?' I wanted to know.

'Oh, her little place is still there, and so is she. Funny, isn't it? I did once think ... you know. She was a looker all right. And you should see her now. Built like a brick outhouse, begging your pardon, gents, where the wife's kept her looks all the time.'

Holmes's mouth twitched. 'The consequence of twenty years of pie and mash, perhaps?' he suggested. 'Well, Lestrade, I am inclined to agree that this has no bearing on the other matter, and is best forgotten.'

Lestrade looked considerably relieved at this, and sat looking out of the window until we reached Baker Street. We had scarcely set foot inside 221B when Billy, the page boy, rushed out to meet us.

'Inspector Lestrade!' he cried, 'your missus is here, sir, and in a dreadful taking.'

'What, Mrs Lestrade? Where, then?' asked the detective.

'She's in the kitchen, sir, with Mrs Hudson,' and Billy led Lestrade off into dark regions where Holmes and I dared not follow.

'I wonder what is amiss?' I mused.

'Doubtless we shall learn soon enough,' said Holmes. He glanced at the door through which Lestrade and Billy had just left. 'What think you to this other business?' he asked me.

'What, this Bessie? Lestrade seems to think it can be dismissed with an easy word, and I'm sure that it can. But I fear his enemies may not see it in that light.'

'Indeed not,' said Holmes. 'They are sure to say that here is the reason for his inefficiency, whether he was chasing this other woman, or merely anxious at being deserted ... even temporarily ... by his wife, that is why he did not give the Clayton matter due attention.'

'You are right,' said I. 'Anyone but a policeman would have had sympathy for his troubles, but we both know that men like Lestrade are expected to rise above things which would reduce any other man to tears. It is most unfair, but a sad fact.'

'Yes ... ah, Lestrade,' said Holmes, as the little detective emerged from the kitchen. 'Nothing wrong, I trust?'

'The wife's upset, as the lad said, sir,' said Lestrade bleakly. He held out a grubby piece of paper. 'This arrived at dinner time, after I'd left, someone pushed it under the door and then knocked, so the wife naturally went to see what it was.'

Holmes read the note with some distaste, and passed it to me. 'Anonymous, of course,' he said.

The note had evidently been written by some uneducated person; the language was vile and the sentiment worse. I handed it back to Holmes.

'Well, the wife read that,' Lestrade went on, 'and she thought … you know. But she's no coward, isn't Violet, and she goes to the door to see if she can see who it was that wrote that. And then …' and he broke off.

'Well?' said Holmes.

'Filth, Mr Holmes, on the very doorstep. A dead cat. And worse.'

'Good Lord!' said I. 'No wonder Mrs Lestrade was upset.'

'She knew I was here, and came round at once. Mrs Hudson has been looking after her, for which I'm very grateful,' said Lestrade. He looked worried. 'But what's to be done, I don't know.'

'Who do you imagine has done this?' Holmes asked.

'Clayton, maybe. Him, or some of his fancy friends, who are probably not so particular as they like to pretend. Either that,' said Lestrade, 'or some of the local lads who I've put away. Everybody knows about my spot of trouble, and there's always those who'll delight in kicking a man when he's down.'

'Not one of the local lads, I think,' said Holmes, 'for all that the writing looks unpolished. The spelling is wrong, but the syntax is perfect.'

'Mr Holmes?'

'I beg your pardon, Lestrade. I was looking at it purely as an intellectual problem, and quite forgetting the distress it has caused your wife. Why not get out of London for a while?' said Holmes. 'Watson here would prescribe the shingle of Southend, I think.'

'Southsea, Holmes,' said I. 'But there are only three letters between them, and, since you mention Southend, I recall that one of Mrs Hudson's cronies has a lodging house there. Mrs Turner, who, you will recall, owned this house before Mrs Hudson. A pleasant enough establishment, the "Bide A Wee Guest House" by name.'

Lestrade shuddered.

'It is clean,' said I. 'And cheap. And the food is excellent, particularly breakfast, what with Mrs Turner's being a Scotchwoman. And more to the point, it is quiet, being out of season.'

'Capital!' said Holmes. 'What say you, Lestrade?'

'Well, I could do with a rest from all this upset, and that's a fact. And the wife, she needs a break. Do you know, Doctor, I think I'll take your advice.'

The matter was quickly arranged, and the Lestrades left for Southend the following day. Holmes and I discussed the matter, but could not see what we might do that would help Lestrade in the least. Holmes eventually gave the matter up, saying that he had other business in hand just at the moment. Frankly, I strongly suspected that he was more or less washing his hands of Lestrade, and equally frankly I could not blame him, for it all seemed very dismal, and it did not look as if all our efforts could produce any gleam of light. Only one very remote possibility suggested itself to my mind, and by the time that occurred it was too late for me to do anything about it, although I resolved to follow up that particular clue as soon as may be.

Late in the evening of the day after the Lestrades had left London, there came a knock at our door, and Inspector Alec MacDonald came in. Holmes and I greeted him warmly, for he was an old friend, but MacDonald was in no mood to spend time on idle conversation. 'The next-door neighbours told me that Inspector Lestrade is off on a little holiday,' he began, 'but they had not his address. I wondered, since he is by way of being a friend of yours, if you knew his whereabouts?'

'Watson, I think, can supply the information you seek,' said Holmes.

'Aye.' MacDonald looked embarrassed. 'The thing is ... you'll be well aware that Inspector Lestrade is in a spot of bother over this Clayton business?'

'We are,' said Holmes.

'Aye. Well, it's like this, Mr Holmes, there's a spot of bother. We've had a report of a missing boy, a lad of seven, in the East End.'

'Good Lord!' said I.

MacDonald nodded. 'My sentiments exactly,' he said drily. 'Now, it would be bad enough in the ordinary way of things, but, as it is ...'

'Just so,' said Holmes.

'I went round to Lestrade's house, as I say, to tip him the wink, unofficial, like, since I know that he'll want to know about it, but of course he's away. He should by rights have left a forwarding address at the Yard, but I expect he was too flustered. So, I thought, with you being friends of his ...'

'You wish us to inform him?' I asked.

'It would be a kindness, sir.'

'Who is in charge of the case?' Holmes put in.

'I have been put in charge of it myself. But I thought perhaps a telegram from you ...'

But Holmes was already scribbling furiously on a telegraph pad, and calling for the page boy.

Five

'Will you come with me, Mr Holmes? And you too, Doctor?' Lestrade looked anxiously from one to the other of us.

It was mid-morning on the day after MacDonald had called upon us. Holmes had sent his telegram late the previous evening. Lestrade had, he told me, received it just as he was about to go to bed, and had taken the first train he could catch in the morning, after, as he put it, tossing and turning all night with devil a wink of sleep.

Holmes had been out on some mysterious errand when Lestrade first arrived, and the detective had fretted abominably until my friend returned. Now Holmes, who had not had time to remove his hat and coat, looked at Lestrade and asked, 'And what exactly would you want us to do?'

'Just back me up, Mr Holmes. That's all. You, and Doctor Watson here, are well enough known at the Yard. If I can say that you have agreed to work alongside me, that will carry a great deal of weight.'

'You really intend to confront the assistant commissioner?' said Holmes.

'I do, sir. Confront him, and ask to be reinstated, to be put back on duty. No, not ask, but demand! Aye, and demand to be put in charge of the case, what's more. It's my case, when all's said and done, for I'm the only man still alive and on the force who was involved in the earlier business.'

'You are sure that Clayton is at the back of this latest disappearance?' asked Holmes.

Lestrade nodded. 'Certain sure, Mr Holmes.'

I said, 'It might be mere coincidence, Lestrade.'

'Coincidence be damned! Begging your pardon, Doctor Watson, but I know this rogue Clayton. If it's not him then my name's not Lestrade, and that's an end of it.'

'Watson is right, I think,' said Holmes calmly. 'This fellow Clayton would, after all, be rather foolish to resume his old ways so soon after his release and the concomitant fuss, and especially with the eyes of the world upon him, as it were. And that is to assume that he was guilty in the earlier case.'

'Ah,' said Lestrade, 'but that's his way, sir. I told you he was cocksure. This is exactly the sort of thing he would do, thumb his nose at those who have trusted him. Rub it in, so to speak.'

Holmes shook his head. 'I can think offhand of at least six explanations for the boy's disappearance,' said he.

Lestrade stared at him. 'Six? And how many of those would involve Clayton?'

'Well, two,' said Holmes reluctantly. He added quickly, 'But they are perhaps the least likely two.'

'Be that as it may,' said Lestrade stubbornly, 'I want to take over this case.'

Holmes shrugged. 'If you are set on it,' said he, 'Watson and I shall certainly do what we can to assist you.'

'I shall send Billy for a cab,' I said.

On the short drive to Scotland Yard, Holmes asked Lestrade, 'Has Mrs Lestrade returned to London with you?'

Lestrade shook his head. 'She said she could not face what might happen, sir, and I cannot say that I blame her. Indeed, I can't say I relish the thought of staying in the house by myself. Not that I'm a coward, if it were a matter of fists or boots in broad daylight, I'd have no hesitation, for that's all part of the job. But this other business, nasty anonymous letters, foul stuff left on your doorstep, and what have you, it unnerves you, and there's no denying that.'

'Why not stay with us?' I suggested.

'Oh, I couldn't think of any such thing.'

'Nonsense,' said Holmes. 'Watson is right, as usual. You must bring your traps along to 221B, as soon as may be.'

'You have no room.'

'You can use one of the lumber rooms.'

'If you don't mind being surrounded by old newspapers,' I added.

'Oh, Billy can do something with them, I am sure, for he is an enterprising lad. Anyway, you evidently find the newspapers comfortable enough,' said Holmes, 'for I found you asleep on top of them last week.'

'Stuff and nonsense, Holmes! I was merely resting after spending a hectic morning looking up an old report. No, it would make but a poor lodging up there, I fear.'

'Well, then, perhaps Lestrade could share with you *pro tem*?

'As soon as we return, I shall give Billy a hand to clear a space upstairs,' said I hastily.

'That is quite settled, then,' said Holmes, 'and we shall expect you this evening, Lestrade. Ah, here we are,' he went on, as the cab drew up outside the familiar building.

I had not previously had the opportunity to see Lestrade in what I might call his natural element. I have some vague recollection that Holmes once described him as being tenacious as a lobster, and I now had a chance to see that tenacity in action. Lestrade blustered, and bullied, and wheedled, and cajoled, and within ten minutes he, Holmes, MacDonald and I were all ushered in to the august presence of the assistant commissioner.

'What's all this about, Lestrade?' asked the assistant commissioner. He was one of the old-school, a former military man with a back like a ramrod and a tiny, stubby moustache which he stroked frequently as an aid to thought, unless perhaps he was a student of Epicurean speculative philosophy and wanted to encourage its growth. 'What the devil are you doing here?'

'I want to be put on to this case of the boy who has vanished,' said Lestrade bluntly.

'Oh? And how the devil d'you know anyone has vanished? The matter has been kept quiet. Or at least, such were my instructions.'

'Mr Sherlock Holmes ...'

'Ah.' The assistant commissioner's tone lost some of its abrasive quality. 'We know you, of course, Mr Holmes.' He looked at MacDonald. 'Though I cannot imagine how you come to know of this matter. Still, that's neither here nor there.' His gaze moved back to Lestrade. 'And why should I put you in charge of the case? I understand that MacDonald here has already been told that it is his case?'

'There's not a better man on the force than Alec MacDonald, sir,' said Lestrade, 'but, and with the greatest possible respect to him, and to you, he was not involved in the original case, and I was.'

'You think this has something to do with Clayton, then?' asked the assistant commissioner.

'I think it has everything to do with him, sir.'

'H'mm.' The assistant commissioner tapped upon his blotter with a silver pencil. 'You'll be aware that some harsh things have already been said in the newspapers about our handling of the Clayton case?'

'I am well aware of it, sir.'

'And you are further aware that if this new business is not properly handled it will blow up in all our faces?'

'I am, sir.'

The assistant commissioner tapped his pencil on the blotter again. 'What say you to all this, MacDonald?'

'It might be a very nasty business, sir, whether Clayton is involved or no. The disappearance of a child, and all. I cannot say that I would exactly fight Inspector Lestrade for the privilege of being in charge of the case.'

'A canny summing-up.' The assistant commissioner tapped his pencil one last time, and came to a sudden decision. 'Very well. You, Lestrade, are in charge of the case, and you, MacDonald, will work with him, and to his instructions, when needed. Is that agreeable to you both?'

'It is, sir,' said MacDonald.

And Lestrade, delighted, said, 'Thank you, sir.'

'Mind you, Lestrade,' the assistant commissioner went on, 'if there is any nonsense about this case, any criticism in the newspapers or anything, I shall prepare the charges against you myself.'

As we left the assistant commissioner's office, Lestrade asked MacDonald, 'You really have no objection to my being in charge of the case?'

'Indeed not,' answered MacDonald with a wry smile. 'As I told the chief, it is likely to prove an awkward business. Not the sort of case that would enhance a man's reputation.'

'And mine is already sufficiently tarnished that it cannot get worse?' said Lestrade.

MacDonald gave an embarrassed laugh. 'I would not have said as much.' He became business-like. 'What are your instructions, Inspector?'

'What other cases have you in hand at the moment?'

'Nothing very pressing, or not compared with this. There has been a spate of puzzling robberies, all evidently by the same person, that's clear enough, but with a great disparity in what has been taken. Valuable stuff one day, and just rubbish the next, with no rhyme or reason to it.'

'H'mm.' Lestrade thought. 'That sounds as if it should be something I know about, but I can't quite bring the facts to mind. Still, that's nothing compared with this other business, so we'll leave that for the time being, and concentrate on this matter of the missing boy. Is that agreeable to you?'

'It is,' said MacDonald.

'First and foremost, then, I want that scoundrel Clayton brought in.'

MacDonald stared at him. 'D'you think that's altogether a wise thing to do, Inspector? The affair is surely dangerous enough as it is?'

'That's as maybe,' said Lestrade stubbornly. 'It's my neck on the chopping block, so I may as well be hung for a sheep as a lamb.'

'Something of a mixed metaphor there, Lestrade,' I protested.

He regarded me with some irritation. 'That being the case,' he continued, 'I'd be grateful, Inspector MacDonald, if you would feel Clayton's collar for me. Just you fetch him along, and we'll ask him to give an account of himself. Keep him snug and safe in a cell until I return. I'm off to see the lad's family, and it will do Clayton no harm to think about what he wants to tell us.'

'I must tell you,' said MacDonald, 'that I have already had Clayton followed.'

'Oh?' This was clearly news to Lestrade. 'And why, pray?'

'Just out of interest,' said MacDonald, almost defensively.' I was by no means satisfied with what I read of the old case,' he went on. 'Were it my case, I doubt if it would have come to court, and that's a fact. But for all that, I'm a policeman too, and I don't like some of the things that have been said in the papers about you, Inspector Lestrade. So, I thought it as well to detail one of my men to keep an eye on Clayton.'

'And?'

'And he reports that the fellow's done nothing at all suspicious.'

'Has your man kept a constant watch, then?' asked Lestrade.

MacDonald shook his head. 'I could not spare more than the one man, and naturally he cannot keep watch every hour of the day.'

'Then, despite your advice, which I value, and your help and solicitude, which I value even more, I'd be grateful if you could bring Clayton in,' said Lestrade, after a moment's thought. 'Be polite to him if you wish, but I'd like a word.'

MacDonald shrugged. 'As you wish.' He nodded to Holmes and me, and went on his way.

'After all,' said Lestrade more calmly, 'Clayton has had his say, and now it's my turn. If nothing else, we can at least eliminate him from our enquiries. Will you come along and see the boy's parents?'

Holmes nodded, and Lestrade hailed a cab. As we set off for the East End, Lestrade asked Holmes, 'You mentioned five or six possible explanations for the boy's disappearance, Mr Holmes?'

'I did. Firstly, of course, there is the possibility that he has vanished more or less legitimately, he has run away from home, or met with an accident. That is surely the most likely explanation?'

'Coincidence, if it were so,' Lestrade pointed out.

'Ah, but life is full of coincidences. Ask Watson, his stories are almost entirely dependent upon them!'

'Be that as it may,' said Lestrade, 'it is odd that the boy should choose to run away just now. However, it is, as you say, an obvious possibility, and it is one which we have not dismissed. In fact, I have a couple of sergeants and a dozen constables standing ready to make house to house enquiries, knock on all the doors in the neighbourhood, should it prove necessary.'

'That is as well,' said Holmes.

'And your other theories?' asked Lestrade, with a wink at me.

'Well,' Holmes went on, 'there is the possibility that Clayton is indeed, as you seem to think, involved. Now, that does strike me as a monstrous coincidence. He is surely not so full of his own cleverness that he would risk drawing attention to himself by resuming his old ways ... assuming for one moment that they were his old ways. The appeal court thought they were not, remember.'

Lestrade gave a grunt of annoyance. 'It has something to do with him, mark my words,' said he.

'I agree that it may,' said Holmes, 'although not in the way you mean.'

'How, then?'

'Well, does it not occur to you that Clayton, or some of his "decadent" friends, may have arranged for the boy to be taken and hidden away safely somewhere, precisely so that you would arrest Clayton? There is the matter of that vile note, which was, I assure you, written by an educated man pretending to be all but illiterate. Then, when Clayton shows conclusively that he was elsewhere at the time the boy vanished, you will be left looking even more ... that is to say, left looking ridiculous. He is sure to have an iron-clad, copper-bottomed, watertight alibi, mark my words. A nautical metaphor for you there, Watson,' he added.

'And what if Clayton knows nothing about what his so-called friends have done on his behalf?' I asked.

'The end result is the same,' said Holmes, 'save that Clayton cannot be touched, even for obstructing the police.'

'I had not thought of that,' confessed Lestrade. 'But you are right, Mr Holmes. That is exactly the sort of thing that the devious little ... fellow ... or maybe some of his friends, would dream up.'

'And did you not also mention another man, the father of one of the boys who vanished twenty years back?' said Holmes. 'Might he not have taken this latest victim, in order to cast suspicion upon Clayton?'

'Good Lord!' said Lestrade. 'Tatton, yes. I hadn't thought of him, but now you mention him, it's true that he was very much down on Clayton. Well, I'll have him brought in as well.'

The cab turned into the maze of narrow streets and alleys that lies between Commercial Road and the Ratcliff Highway, and stopped at the entrance to a little court. 'Can't get the cab in there, gents,' the driver told us.

Lestrade got down. 'Wait here,' he told the cabbie, and led the way into the court. A uniformed constable, looking ill at ease in those uncongenial surroundings, stood by a door. 'She's upset, sir,' he ventured as Lestrade approached.

'Oh? And who asked you?' Lestrade pushed open the door and entered without knocking or other preamble.

The room in which we found ourselves evidently did duty as kitchen, dining room and parlour ... aye, and probably bathroom, too, on very infrequent occasions. It was only a small room, and it seemed already full to capacity. Two women, both with red eyes, sat at a small deal table, while two or three ragged children, between the ages of one and three, played on the floor. As Lestrade made his way inside, all the occupants of the room glanced up at us.

'And who are you?' demanded the younger of the women. She was perhaps thirty, but bore the marks of a harsh life alongside the temporary signs of grief. She must once have been attractive, I thought; her colouring, which had not yet quite surrendered to the London atmosphere, together with her accent, spoke of Ireland's greenery, and I wondered how she came to be here, among the smoke and grime of the East End.

'Police,' said Lestrade shortly. 'Mrs Bates, is it?'

'I'm Mrs Bates,' said the younger woman. 'This is my friend, Maggie.'

Lestrade nodded. Maggie got up, made a curious bobbing motion that may have been intended for a curtsey, and ushered the children into an inner chamber.

'Sit down, please,' said Mrs Bates. 'I'm forgetting my manners.'

'Very understandable, madam,' said Holmes in a soothing tone, as we found chairs.

'Now then, Mrs Bates,' said Lestrade, 'You reported your son missing, I think?'

Mrs Bates nodded, without speaking.

'Last night, that was?'

Another nod.

'And when did you see him last?'

'Yesterday evening, sir. I sent to him the corner for a ... well, for a jug of beer, for supper, you know. He went out right as rain, and never come back.'

'What time was that?' asked Lestrade.

'Oh, about six o'clock.'

'And when did you raise the alarm?'

'Well, sir, I was busy, you know, what with the other kiddies, and my husband, so it wasn't for a while that I missed him. Then I thought, you know, that he might just be playing outside. And then ...' and a sob finished he sentence.

'Was there any reason that you can think of why he should run away?' asked Holmes.

Mrs Bates looked at him blankly.

'He had not been scolded for being naughty, let us say?' Holmes went on.

Mrs Bates flushed. 'No. Not scolded, sir. No.'

'Come, now,' said Lestrade. 'We can hardly help if you do not tell us what we want to know.'

Mrs Bates wiped the back of a hand over the general area of eyes and nose. 'Well, sir, it's like this. Mr Bates, he's not … that is … he's not Alfie's father.'

'Oh?' said Lestrade.

Defensively, Mrs Bates said, 'I'm what they call his "common law" wife, see? That means …'

'We know well enough what it means,' said Lestrade. 'And this Bates had done what? Scolded the lad, that it?'

'It's difficult for Bates, sir. You know, when Alfie's cheeky, and Bates tries to correct him, then "You're not my dad!" is what he gets from Alfie. I try, God knows, but …'

'And yesterday?' said Holmes.

'Well, sir, there had been a bit … a little bit of shouting and what have you, earlier on. But that was all blown over by supper time, I'll swear to that.'

'Where does this Bates work?' asked Lestrade.

'The leather warehouse, sir, by the river.'

'I know it. He'll be there now?'

'Yes, sir. He was frantic about Alfie, of course, but he doesn't get paid if he doesn't go to work. What can you do?'

'It is difficult,' said Holmes. 'It is a delicate question, I know, but what of the boy's natural father? What is his name, and where may he be found?'

'His name's O'Connor, sir. Last I knew, he was working in the brewery at Seven Dials, but that was a few years ago.'

Holmes nodded. 'Try not to be too despondent, Mrs Bates. The inspector here will put his best men on to finding your son.'

'Thank you, sirs.' Mrs Bates hesitated, and then, as we rose to leave, she asked, 'You don't think he has anything to do with it? That man who was just out of prison? Only Maggie was saying …'

'There!' said Lestrade, with a triumphant glance at Holmes. He laid his hand on Mrs Bates' arm with considerably more gentleness than he had shown thus far. 'Don't you worry, dear,' he told her, 'we're already looking into that.'

As we went out into what served the inhabitants of that dreary region for daylight, there was a sort of subdued muttering, and I noticed a small knot of people standing round the court. Lestrade nodded at them. 'Same as last time,' said he. 'The news has soon got round, you see.' He walked over to the crowd, and in a loud voice told them, 'We'll do what's necessary. You go home, and let us get on with it.'

This was not what the little crowd wanted to hear, and there was a certain amount of grumbling, although they seemed not entirely antagonistic. After a few more words from Lestrade, they began to disperse.

Lestrade came back to us. 'A bad business,' said he. 'If we don't find something soon, they'll be after taking the law into their own hands, and there's no telling what unpleasantness might arise.' He asked the young constable, 'Did you ask at the pub if they'd seen the lad?'

'Yes, sir, but they hadn't. He had evidently never got that far.'

'H'mm. And what about the neighbours?'

'Nothing as far as I could see. I didn't get the chance to ask properly. And in any case a lot of them round here aren't exactly friendly to us, sir, as you know. Some of 'em just won't talk to us.'

'Well, they'll bloody well have to!' said Lestrade with some warmth. 'Look, get out of here, find Sergeant Miller, he's expecting to hear from me, and say that I want every house, every tenement, visited. I want to know if anyone round here can tell us anything at all.'

'Sir.' The constable saluted, and went off.

'It looks as if we have another possibility for your list, Holmes,' said I as we got back into the cab.

'What, the natural father? Yes, indeed.'

'You think the boy may have gone off to try and find his real father?' said Lestrade.

'That, or the natural father may have decided to come and take the boy away. That would be quite understandable, would it not?'

'H'mm.' Lestrade thought a moment. 'Would we be better trying to see this O'Connor, think you?'

'We must certainly try,' said Holmes. 'But Mrs Bates was vague as to where he might be, and moreover, if he has taken the boy, he may well be on his way back to Dublin or somewhere now. The leather factory is nearer, so let us see this Bates first, then continue on to Seven Dials and try to track down the other one.'

'Right enough,' and Lestrade called out an order to the cabbie.

Six

The leather warehouse was a great, gloomy place, and the air was heavy with the pungent but invigorating smell of oak bark. Lestrade quickly found the foreman, and asked for Bates to be sent to see us.

Bates proved to be a sturdy fellow, somewhat above middle height and with great broad shoulders on him. He looked anxiously at Lestrade. 'Found the boy, have you?'

'Not yet. We wished to ask you a few questions.'

'Me? I don't know nothing about it. I wasn't even in the house when the missus sent him to the pub.'

'No?'

'I was still here. You can ask the foreman. He was gone, gone out of the house, I mean, by the time I got home. Then it was a while before we got worried, like.'

'I see. Now, then, had there been any sort of argument, a quarrel, anything of that sort earlier yesterday?'

'No more than usual. Alfie, he gets a bit out of hand sometimes, on account ...' and he broke off, and stared at the ground.

'Mrs Bates told us how matters stood,' said Holmes gently.

'Ah. Well, gents, you know how it is. Alfie gets a bit cheeky, sometimes, like I say, but nothing too bad. Matter of fact, I almost like him better than my own kids, he's a cheerful little devil, gives as good as he gets, and I like that.' He turned his head away from us, and coughed noisily to hide his emotions.

'And yesterday?' asked Lestrade.

Bates looked at him and shrugged. 'We'd had a bit of a barney in the morning. I was up late, I'm usually gone by the time the kids are up, and he was cheeky. Gave him the back of my hand, but nothing serious.'

'Nothing that would make him run away?' asked Lestrade.

Bates shook his head. 'Never run away before, has he? And we've argued plenty of times.'

'Now,' said Lestrade, 'this is a bit awkward, but do you know the lad's natural father?'

'Never seen him, as far as I know. That was all over when the missus and me first took up. I wasn't to blame for them splitting up, or anything.'

'I see. Does the boy talk about him at all? What I mean is, would he run off to see him? Has he ever done that, or talked about it?'

'Never.'

'And the father has never threatened to come and take the boy, nothing like that?'

'Nothing like that. Matter of fact, I think he was kind of grateful to me, you know, taking the boy off his hands, as it were.'

'Well,' said Lestrade, 'so far we've discovered nothing. But I'm sure it'll all come right, so don't you worry too much.'

'No.' Bates hesitated. 'But some of the lads were saying that that bloke ... you know, the one who was in clink for them others, a few years ago ... they say he's on the loose again.'

'You may be certain we have our eye on him,' said Lestrade.

'I'm sure you have, Inspector. Only ... well, you do wonder, don't you?'

Holmes said, 'Tell me, Mr Bates, did Alfie know where you work?'

'Yes, sir. Of course.'

'This place is no very great distance from your house. I wonder if he could perhaps have set off in this direction, intending to meet you as you came home?'

'Bates looked doubtful. 'I suppose he might,' he agreed.

'But he never has before?' asked Lestrade.

'No, sir.'

'Thank you, Bates, that was all.' Lestrade laid a friendly hand on Bates' broad shoulder. 'Try not to brood about it too much.'

Bates nodded without any real conviction, and went back to his work.

'I'll join you in a moment,' Lestrade told us, and wandered off in the same direction as that just taken by Bates.

Holmes and I returned to the cab. 'This fellow seems genuine enough,' said I.

'He does. But that is not an infallible guarantee, is it? Ah, here is Lestrade.'

'The foreman confirms that Bates was here until six,' said Lestrade. 'Nothing there, then, is there, Mr Holmes?'

'It would appear not.'

'Seven Dials next, then?' said Lestrade, and he called an order to the cabbie.

As we rattled back through the squalid streets from whence we had just come, Lestrade recognized a familiar face, and halted the cab whilst he spoke to a uniformed sergeant, who told us that the search had begun in earnest.

'Every house, mind,' Lestrade reminded him. 'And all empty premises, too, because he may well have slipped in somewhere for the night and got trapped or something.'

'Very well, sir,' said the sergeant. 'But I don't like the fact that we're so close to the river. If he went down there, and got into trouble, there's no telling how long he'd be there before someone spotted him,' and he looked worried.

'Best alert the river police,' said Lestrade. 'Though I'm sure they'd have told us if they'd found anyone.'

We spent the rest of the journey in a gloomy silence, each of us busy with his own thoughts. The cab rattled along until we reached the insalubrious area of Seven Dials, worse by far than the East End from whence we had come, and halted before the great gates with the stone leopard atop them.

Once again, Lestrade sought out someone in authority, and determined that O'Connor did still work there. Before very long, O'Connor himself came out to meet us. He was a cheery looking soul, and he shook our hands heartily. 'I hear you're wanting to see me?' he said.

'Police,' said Lestrade.

'Oh?' O'Connor looked puzzled, but unworried; if he were acting, then it was well done. 'And why would you want to see me?'

'You have a son, I understand? Alfred?'

'Alfie? That I have. Wait though, has something happened to the lad?'

'He's vanished,' said Lestrade.

'How d'you mean?' O'Connor looked as puzzled as before, and again it seemed genuine enough to me.

'Just what I say,' said Lestrade. 'He's disappeared. Went out on an errand and never came back.'

O'Connor shook his head without speaking.

'When did you last set eyes on him?' asked Lestrade.

'I'm not sure I could tell you. Two years? Maybe more. His mother and myself, we didn't exactly see eye to eye, we had our differences, and I ... well, I moved on, as you might say. Then she took up with some other fellow, and that was that.'

'So, it's a couple of years since you saw him? And you haven't tried to see him?'

O'Connor gave a sort of defensive shrug. 'It wouldn't have been altogether befitting, would it? The other fellow in the house, and all? No, I wished them luck and left them to it.'

'And the boy has never come to see you?'

'No. No doubt his mother thought it best that he should regard the other fellow as his father. Very understandable, don't you think?'

'Never mind what I think,' said Lestrade. 'Where are you living at the moment?'

'Just down the street. I can tell you the address if you like. But why would you ask that?'

'You won't mind if we take a quick look at your lodgings?'

'Not a bit. Though you'll not find anything there. Wait, though! You weren't thinking the boy might be there, were you?'

'Just an ordinary precaution,' said Lestrade. 'Now, where were you last night, about six o'clock?'

'I was here. You can ask the foreman.'

'I will.'

O'Connor gave us his address, and after Lestrade had confirmed that he had indeed been at work the previous evening, we visited O'Connor's lodging, but without any outcome. There was no sign of anything untoward, and the other inhabitants all swore that O'Connor would never harm a fly, that is unless he were the worse for drink. 'And that's pretty often, I imagine,' said Lestrade sourly. 'These fellows get a regular allowance from the brewery, you know.'

'Be that as it may,' said Holmes, 'we have no reason to suspect that either of these men has anything to hide.'

'No, we haven't,' said Lestrade. 'And that being the case, I propose that we return to the Yard, and have a friendly little chat with the one man who I think does have something to hide. Our friend Clayton.' And he gave us a lead by climbing back inside the cab.

At Scotland Yard, Lestrade paused to speak to a uniformed sergeant. 'Get one of your lads to call upon Tatton,' he told him. 'You know, the fellow who keeps threatening Clayton? He's been arrested a few times, so you'll find his address soon enough.'

The sergeant nodded, and went off. Lestrade then sought out MacDonald, who was looking very worried. 'Did you bring Clayton in?' asked Lestrade.

'I did. Together with his solicitor.'

'Oh?'

'The two of them were together when I got there,' said MacDonald, 'and the solicitor chap insisted on accompanying his client.'

'We'll see about that,' said Lestrade grimly. 'Where are they?'

'In the interview room.'

'Not a cell?'

'The solicitor said that unless I was arresting Clayton, he wouldn't have him in a cell.'

Lestrade sighed. He led us down a dingy corridor and stopped before a door, the paint of which was in a somewhat distressed condition. He threw open the door without ceremony, and led the way inside.

Clayton was lounging at a table, talking to another man. As we entered the room, this second man rose greet us. He was a young man, somewhat below the middle height, and dressed so very fashionably as to be almost a caricature of the current style.

'Who are you?' asked Lestrade in his blunt way.

'My name is Augustus Hector Wickham-Montrose.'

'Blimey!' said Lestrade involuntarily.

'It often provokes that reaction,' said the young man. Under some circumstances I might have admired him for that response, but his delivery was so offensively listless, so clearly intended to show that Lestrade was a lesser mortal who must be put firmly in his place, that the words had the effect of making me take an instant dislike to the man. He produced a silver card case, and handed a card to Lestrade. 'You will observe that I am a solicitor,' he said, 'and Mr Clayton here is my client. There will therefore, I trust, be no objection to my remaining here whilst you speak to him?'

'I'd rather you didn't,' Lestrade told him.

MacDonald added hastily, 'It is merely a matter of a few simple questions, sir.'

'Then there should be no objection to my being here?' the solicitor, whose name was so lengthy that I had forgotten it, asked Lestrade. He glanced at Holmes, and went on, 'I have already made the acquaintance of Inspector MacDonald, but may I ask who these gentleman may be?'

'This is Mr Sherlock Holmes, and this is Doctor Watson.'

'Ah. I know them by reputation, of course.'

'They are assisting us in this matter,' said Lestrade.

'In what capacity, pray?'

Lestrade was thrown by this. 'Well, as …'

The lawyer broke in, 'Mr Holmes's reputation is, of course, excellent. And we have all heard of Doctor Watson. But they are none the less merely private citizens. If anyone is to be summarily ejected from the proceedings, I suggest it should be Mr Holmes and Doctor Watson.'

'Look here, Mr ...' Lestrade's memory was evidently as faulty as my own, for he had to consult the card in his hand before going on, 'Mr Wickham-Montrose, I must tell you that Mr Holmes ...'

Clayton, who thus far had neither spoken nor stood up, now tugged at Wickham-Montrose's arm, and said, 'Leave it, Gussie. I don't care how many of them there are. I've nothing to hide, as you know. In fact, I'd rather these others stayed. They can act as witnesses.' He leered at Holmes and me, and went on, 'And I assure you, gentlemen, that you will be needed as such.'

'Enough of that!' Lestrade told him.

Wickham-Montrose raised a hand. 'Gentlemen, gentlemen, please. I am certain this could all be resolved amicably.'

'You are right, sir,' added Holmes.

Lestrade subsided. 'Very well,' said he. He looked at Clayton. 'Where were you yesterday evening?' he demanded.

'And why should ...' Clayton broke off at a look from Wickham-Montrose. 'Should I answer?' he asked the solicitor.

'By all means.'

'Very well, then. Yesterday afternoon I was with some friends, including Gussie, that is, Mr Wickham-Montrose here. We had dinner at seven or so, and broke up at around ten in the evening.' Is that right?' he asked Wickham-Montrose.

'Quite right. I can swear to that, Inspector, and so can half a dozen others.'

Lestrade was momentarily at a loss, then he asked, 'Have you ever heard of a boy called Alfred Bates?'

Clayton looked at the solicitor. Wickham-Montrose lifted one shoulder slightly, nothing so uncouth as a shrug, and said, 'You may answer.'

'Never heard of him,' said Clayton. 'Why do you ask? Oh, I see.' He sneered at Lestrade. 'This lad gone missing, has he? And so naturally your first thought was of me. How sweet!'

'Enough of your lip,' said Lestrade, holding himself in with an obvious effort. He looked at Holmes, an odd light in his eyes. 'Well, unless you have any questions, Mr Holmes?'

Holmes shook his head.

'In that case,' Lestrade told Clayton, 'you can clear off. I've finished with you.'

'Oh? But I haven't finished with you, you may be sure of that.'

Wickham-Montrose laid a restraining arm on Clayton's sleeve. 'What my client means,' said he carefully, 'is that we shall be lodging a formal protest at this unwarranted persecution, which will, I assure you, do considerable damage to your already weak situation.'

'Oh, yes?' Lestrade tried to brazen it out, but it sounded hollow. Clayton and his solicitor rose and marched out without further comment. Lestrade mopped his brow. 'Well,' said he without any real conviction, 'there's always Tatton. Let's hope that he proves more helpful.'

'Let us hope so,' murmured Holmes.

'Aye,' added MacDonald heavily. 'I'll check just now, see if there's any sign of the man.' He left without further remark.

Lestrade, evidently feeling the urge to talk, said, 'MacDonald seems to think I'm not handling this very well. And I have to say he's probably right.'

Holmes made no answer, and I could think of none, so the three of us sat there in silence for what seemed an age. I was relieved when MacDonald eventually put his head round the door and announced, 'Tatton is in the other room, Inspector.'

'Quick work,' said I.

'Oh, we know him quite well,' said MacDonald. 'The constable tried his place of work first off, and he was there. He's a traveller for a firm of wine and spirit merchants, and the office is just down the road.' He ushered us into a room almost identical to the one we had just left.

A middle-aged man was sitting at a deal table. He had an anxious expression on his face, which deepened as he saw Lestrade. 'Inspector?' said he. 'What's all this about, then?'

'I'll ask the questions, if you please,' Lestrade told him. He nodded at the man. 'Gentlemen, this is Tatton, of whom I've spoken. This,' he told the frightened man, 'is Mr Sherlock Holmes, and this is Doctor Watson. You'll have heard of them, I'm sure?'

Tatton nodded nervously. 'But why have I been brought here?'

'Where were you last night, around six o'clock?' asked Lestrade without further ado.

'Last night? I was out, working. Out Esher way.'

'And can anyone bear that out?'

Tatton shook his head.

'Well, then, what about your customers?' asked Lestrade. 'I assume you talked to someone?'

'I had a couple of shops to visit,' said Tatton defensively.

'And when was your last appointment?'

'Half past eleven.'

'What, in the morning?'

Tatton nodded.

'And what time did you get home, then?'

Tatton hesitated. 'Let me see. It would be around nine.'

'It doesn't take ten hours to get back from Esher,' Lestrade pointed out. 'Did you go anywhere for a meal?'

Tatton shook his head. 'I had a bit of bread and cheese,' said he. 'I took it along with me, and ate it sitting under a hedge somewhere on the outskirts of the town.' He paused. 'The firm give a daily allowance for meals, see? A fixed allowance.'

'So, you claim the allowance, but don't spend anything?'

Tatton nodded. 'All the fellows do it,' he said.

'And what then?'

'Well, I had the addresses of a couple of prospective clients, so I went along to try to track them down.'

'Can they speak as to that?'

'No. One of the shops was closed, a half day. The other had shut down altogether.'

'And nobody saw you hanging around these places?' Lestrade's voice was sceptical.

Tatton shook his head. 'It was quiet,' said he.

'Very well. I give you an hour to take your luncheon, another to find that your prospective customers were no more. What then?'

Tatton said nothing.

'I say, what then?'

'Well, then, if you must know, I took a walk.'

'It must have been a damned long walk!'

'And what if it was, then?'

Holmes put in gently, 'Mr Tatton, there is a serious reason for these questions. If you have any witnesses who can vouch for your whereabouts, it would be as well to let Inspector Lestrade know their names.'

Tatton, clearly impressed by Holmes's demeanour, answered, 'I can see that, sir. But I really did take a long walk. I was feeling a bit down, what with the two shops being shut and what have you. Inspector Lestrade will have told you how matters stand with me, I'm sure, gentlemen? I get a bit down, sometimes, and need to be alone.'

Holmes nodded. 'I sympathize there,' said he.

'And then I missed the train,' added Tatton with something of an anti-climax. 'I had intended to be back home earlier, but …' and he shrugged his shoulders.

'Well, Inspector?' asked Holmes of Lestrade.

Lestrade shrugged in his turn.

'What's going on?' Tatton wanted to know. 'If you told me, perhaps I could help.'

Holmes looked at Lestrade, who nodded, and said, 'Well, then, my lad, it's this way. A young lad has disappeared, in the East End.'

Tatton groaned. 'And that fellow Clayton just released from clink!' said he. 'I told you no good would come of it. Said it over and over, I have, and who listens?' He paused. 'But why did you want to see me? Here, you didn't think I had anything to do with it, did you?'

'Never you mind,' said Lestrade. 'Sorry to have troubled you. You can go.'

And Tatton, after some grumbling, did go. Scarcely had he left than there was a rattle at the door, and the assistant commissioner, his moustache bristling in an aggressive way, burst in.

'A pretty kettle of fish, this, Lestrade!' said he angrily.

'That it is, sir ...'

'Clayton and his solicitor have lodged a complaint as to your high-handed action. And I am bound to say I cannot entirely blame them. Have you progressed in the slightest since last I spoke to you?'

'No, sir, I have not.'

'In that event,' said the assistant commissioner, 'I shall release the news to the press, and ask them to appeal for information as to the lad's whereabouts.'

'Sir?' Lestrade's voice was pleading. 'If I might have just another day or so?'

'Not another hour. Not another minute.' The assistant commissioner looked at Holmes, and added more calmly, 'We have kept the story quiet until now, Mr Holmes, not wanting everyone to jump to the same silly conclusions as ... that is to say, not wanting people to jump to silly conclusions as to Clayton, and so forth. But the house to house search of the area has proved fruitless. I have just returned from there, and nothing has turned up. And consequently, I have no choice but to ask the press for help.'

'I am sure you are right,' said Holmes.

'As for you, Lestrade,' the assistant commissioner continued, 'you are still in charge of the case, for the time being. When once it is over, we shall have a long chat as to your immediate future.'

There was nothing that Holmes and I could do, so we left discreetly, and returned to Baker Street. Lestrade, looking very abashed, turned up on our doorstep later that evening with a shabby suitcase, and we furnished him with a makeshift bed in a corner of the sitting room.

The story of young Alfred Bates' disappearance, along with his description, appeared prominently in the evening papers. Lestrade read these, shook his head without any remark, and went off, I suspected to visit the local public house. He had not returned by the time I went to bed, and he had gone before I came down to breakfast next day.

The story of young Bates' disappearance figured again in the morning's editions, and Lestrade looked in at ten o'clock to say that there was still no news. I suggested to Holmes that he enlist the help of what he called his irregulars, the ragamuffins and street urchins who had proved so useful in the past, and he agreed. Then, like Lestrade, he disappeared, I assumed to seek the help of these unofficial forces, or otherwise to pursue the investigation, for I did not think that Holmes had anything else in hand at the moment.

Lestrade called upon me again once or twice in the course of the day, still without anything to report, but I saw nothing of Holmes until the early evening, when he appeared, looking exhausted, and gave monosyllabic and unsatisfactory answers to any questions as to his doings.

The story appeared again in the papers that evening, but with less prominence than previously. Holmes read the reports in silence, then eventually said, 'There is one possibility that I scarcely like to think about, of course.'

'And what's that?' asked Lestrade.

'If the boy has not run away, or got lost, and further if neither Clayton nor this Tatton had anything to do with it, then there may be some unknown assailant at large. Perhaps someone else of weak intellect has seen the accounts of the old case, and decided to work independently?'

'Don't, Mr Holmes!' said Lestrade. 'It makes my blood run cold just to think of it.'

By the following morning, the story had been ousted from the front page, and Holmes looked at Lestrade and me and shook his head sadly. But he was wrong in his unspoken surmise, for at nine o'clock that same morning, a young labourer named Albert Sanderson marched into H division police station in Whitechapel carrying in his arms little Alfred Bates, very tired, very dirty, and very frightened; but very much alive.

Seven

'Well, Doctor Watson?' asked Lestrade.

'The boy is in excellent health, although he could do with a good wash,' said I. 'No injuries of any sort. He is very upset and frightened by all the fuss, just as one might have expected, of course, and I doubt if you'll get anything out of him until his mother arrives to comfort him.'

'I told you he was fine,' said Sanderson, with a touch of truculence. He was some eighteen or nineteen years of age, sturdily built and with a generally confident air about him, but just at the moment he looked as if he were a little apprehensive at the publicity he had attracted to himself, and he tried to offset this with a devil-may-care attitude. He sat in the Whitechapel police station, a mug of tea on front of him, while Lestrade, MacDonald, who had brought us the news of the boy's being found that morning, and Sherlock Holmes all sat on the other side of the table and regarded him curiously. I had just examined young Alfred Bates, who was now being cared for by one of the police matrons, and as I have just said, I found that the boy was none the worse for his adventures. I sat down next to Holmes and the others.

'We have to be certain of these things,' said Lestrade. 'Now then, Sanderson, what can you tell us about this business?'

'Nothing,' said Sanderson frankly. 'I found the boy, like I told the sergeant when I come into the station. And again to the inspector here,' with a nod at MacDonald.

'Well, now you can tell me,' said Lestrade.

Sanderson sighed. 'Well, I'd been out last night, on the ... that is, out with some friends. The pub, you know? We kept it up pretty late, I'm afraid, but you know how it is, Inspector? And when I get back home, I'm a bit hazy, you follow? Went straight to bed and off to sleep at once, without even taking my boots off, as you might say. Well, I had to work this morning, the new Underground line, it is, that we're building now, and I was up around half past five, with a head on me like nobody's business. Anyway, that's beside the point. I puts the kettle on, and goes for a loaf a bread out of my little pantry, and there's this noise, see?'

'Noise?'

'A scurrying, scuttling sort of noise. A bit like a rat or a mouse, only this wasn't no rat or mouse. Well, I say I'd a bad head, and I says, "Whoever might be hiding in there had better get the ...", that is to say, I told them to come out of it. And the little chap crawls out from behind the peggy-tub.'

'You knew who he was, then?'

'Not a bit of it. Not then, at any rate. I hadn't seen the newspapers, see? But I could see he was scared, and hungry. He'd gnawed the crust off my loaf while he'd been in there, and eaten most of the cheese, so I gave him some grub, bacon and a cup of tea, and he settled down a bit, and so I was able to ask about him. It appears he'd run away from home, had some sort of quarrel with his old man, his father I mean, and been scared of what would happen when his dad got home. So, he'd run away. Well, I could see what he meant. I've done the self-same thing myself, more than once, and for the same reason.'

'How came he to be lurking in your pantry?' asked Holmes.

'He said he'd spent one night in the street, dozing in a doorway. The next day he felt hungry and scared, too scared to go back home, so he'd looked round, seen my pantry window ajar and crawled in. Helped himself to some bread, and fallen asleep until the evening, when he heard me moving about, getting ready to go out, I expect, and been too scared to move. Had another night's sleep of sorts, and that's when I found him.' He looked anxiously at Lestrade. 'I did the right thing, though, didn't I, Inspector?'

'You did, my lad. And he told you who he was, did he? His name and so forth?'

'Said his name was Alfie. Well, I didn't know what to do for the best. Like I say, I hadn't seen the newspapers, so I didn't know there was all this fuss. Anyway, I took him next door, to see the old dear who lives there, ask her what I should do. She's seen the newspapers, and flew into a tizzy, tells me the police are after him, so I bring him here. And I'm sure I don't know what the foreman will say when I do get to work. Irish, he is, and a real temper with him.'

'If there's any nonsense of that kind,' said Lestrade majestically, 'you just refer him to me, my lad. Well, thank you for your help, and we won't keep you from your work any longer.'

Sanderson nodded, and left, looking none too displeased at being able to leave the atmosphere of officialdom behind him. There followed a long silence, which MacDonald finally broke. 'Well,' said he, looking at Lestrade, 'will you tell the assistant commissioner the good news, or shall I?' He glanced at his watch. 'The boy's mother is being brought here just now to look after him, so we ought to get back to the Yard.'

Lestrade was silent for a moment, then he said, 'If you would be so kind, Inspector, I'd esteem it a great kindness if you could tell the chief. I'm not sure I can face him just at the moment.'

MacDonald nodded sympathetically. 'I quite understand.' He hesitated, then added, 'But he'll be sure to ask to see you.'

'I know that only too well,' said Lestrade. 'And I'll see him, and face the music, all in good time. But not just now.' His voice was almost pleading as he added the last sentence.

MacDonald nodded sympathetically. 'I'll tell him you're pursuing another line of inquiry,' said he.

'Thank you,' said Lestrade. 'Of course, if he asks any awkward questions …'

MacDonald coughed to hide his embarrassment. 'In that case, of course, I'll have no option.' And he stood up and retrieved his hat, and nodded a farewell to us.

'Well, gents,' said Lestrade as the door closed after MacDonald, 'I know it's a bit early in the day, and what have you, but I'm ready for a drink. Doctor? Mr Holmes?'

'We shall gladly accompany you,' said Holmes.

'I know a little place just off Trafalgar Square,' said Lestrade as we climbed into a cab and set off. 'Only a small place, and nothing fancy, but it's quiet, and they do a very decent pint of mild. It suits me, and I go there often … occasionally, that is to say. When I want to drown my sorrows,' he added with a hint of bitterness in his tone.

'Come, now,' Holmes told him, 'do not be too despondent. The boy is safe and well, after all. As for the rest, things may be brighter than you fear.'

'Blotted my copy book good and proper, didn't I?' asked Lestrade.

'In the circumstances, it was a logical course of action. But I was not referring to this business of Clayton, or the missing boy.'

'Oh?' Despite his woes, Lestrade looked interested.

'I have been actively pursuing my own enquiries,' Holmes went on, 'and I have every hope that I may be able to help with the latter case, that of Sir Octavius.'

'Oh?' Lestrade was more than interested now.

Holmes looked at his watch. 'In fact,' said he, 'I have arranged to meet someone at Baker Street at two this afternoon. Trafalgar Square is not too far from our humble lodgings, so I propose that we convert your sorrow-drowning drink into an early luncheon, and then the three of us can go along and see what we shall see.' And he relapsed into silence, refusing to answer the many questions which Lestrade and I very naturally wished to put to him.

We left the cab at the rank in Trafalgar Square, and set off on foot, Lestrade saying that his pub was at no great distance.

The square was crowded, and, as luck would have it, on getting down from the cab I almost literally bumped into an old acquaintance, a man I had not seen since my army days. Lestrade and Holmes murmured a polite greeting when I introduced the three of them, then set off, whilst I exchanged some words of reminiscence with my old friend. By the time we had resolved not to wait so long until we met again, Holmes and Lestrade were some fifty yards ahead of me.

As I turned to follow them, I was aware that something was wrong. I did not see precisely what happened, my mind being still full of the recent conversation with a man I had last seen some twelve or fifteen years back, but I saw Lestrade jostled by a short man, heard the detective cry, 'Hey!' then the short man set off towards me at a run.

I was wondering in a vague sort of way what was amiss, when Lestrade called out, 'Stop, thief!' That was enough for me; I stopped the man by the simple expedient of standing in the path of his headlong flight, and he struck me fair and square.

I have said that he was a short man. He was also a slight man. Indeed, that is something of an understatement; he was a veritable shrimp of a man, it would have taken two or three of him to make a decent jockey. So, although the collision winded me for a moment, it sent him sprawling on the pavement, and by the time he was back on his feet, Holmes and Lestrade had reached us.

'Now, then,' said Lestrade, gripping the little man by the shoulders and turning him round roughly. 'Well, I'm blowed!' he added. 'Frankie. I should have known. Gents, you won't know Frankie, so I'll introduce you. This is Francis Coombes, known to one and all as Frankie, an old friend of mine; Frankie, you've just barged into Doctor John H Watson. And this ...' and Lestrade could hardly contain himself ... 'is Mr Sherlock Holmes.'

'Sherlock 'Olmes! Oh, blimey!' and the poor wretch almost fainted in Lestrade's arms.

'I'll thank you to return my pocketbook,' said Holmes sharply.

'Yours, Holmes?' said I, delighted. 'I was sure it was Lestrade's pocket he'd picked.'

'It'd take a better man than old Frankie here to lift my wallet,' said Lestrade with a grin.

Holmes regarded us with a contemptuous silence. 'Thank you,' said he, as Coombes handed his pocketbook over.

'Well, Frankie,' said Lestrade, 'you've done it this time, my lad. Fancy you being so daft as to pick the pocket of Mr Sherlock Holmes, and with me standing there watching.'

'Honest, Mr Lestrade, I didn't know it was Mr 'Olmes. I never seen him before, did I? If I'd known, I'd never 'ave done anythink like that. And I didn't know it was you either, Mr Lestrade. Honest. I never recognized you, not without your uniform.'

Lestrade sighed theatrically. 'Frankie, Frankie. How long have you known me? Twenty years? And in all that time, have you ever seen me in uniform? I'm a detective, aren't I? A plain-clothes detective. See,' he explained carefully, 'that's what "plain-clothes" means, that I don't wear a uniform. See?'

Coombes's reply to this was a sort of strangled groan.

'And now I come to think of it,' said Lestrade, looking closely at his prisoner, 'there was another little matter. Mr MacDonald was speaking of a spate of puzzling robberies, good stuff one day, rubbish the next. I knew it rang a bell. That was you, Frankie, wasn't it? See,' he added to Holmes and me, 'it was the good stuff being taken that fooled me. If it had been just rubbish, I'd have thought of Frankie right off.' He regarded Coombes with some concern. ''Ere, are you all right?'

'I'm feeling a bit faint, like, Mr Lestrade.'

'Come along, then. In here and have a drink.'

Lestrade escorted the swaying Coombes through the door of the saloon bar, and, with a quick nod at the proprietor, into a back parlour of sorts. 'We'll not be interrupted here,' said the detective, waving us to seats. When the owner had brought us drinks, Lestrade leaned back and regarded Coombes almost with paternal affection. 'Yes,' he repeated with relish, 'done it good and proper this time. What with the robberies, and picking Mr Holmes's pocket. Ten years at least! And a lick of the cat to boot, as like as not.'

Coombes shuddered visibly. 'Ten years, Mr Lestrade? It'll kill me. And what about my old mum? It'll kill her, too. I'm all she's got, you know.'

'You should have thought of that sooner, shouldn't you?' asked Lestrade. His voice was rough, but his gaze betrayed him. He shook his head sadly, and addressed Holmes and me. 'His old man was just the same,' he told us. 'Useless! All the instincts of a tea-leaf, but none of the skill. I arrested him, Frankie's dad, I mean, when I was just a young copper, only a year on the force. In the "Pillars of 'Ercules", it was,' he added reminiscently. 'I'm leaning on the bar, out of uniform, of course, taking a quiet drink, when Frankie's old dad sidles up to me, and talks out of the side of his cake-hole. "Wanna buy a suit, gov'?" says he, running the words all together, as it were. I tell him, I can't afford no suit, not on my wage, though I didn't tell him what I did to earn it, of course. "You can afford this suit", he tells me. "Fell off the back of the cart, didn't it?" and I booked him then and there! Mind you,' he went on, 'it was a lovely suit, and no mistake. Serge, and proper serge it was, too, in them days. You did get some beautiful cloth back then, there's no denying it.'

'I never knew that,' said Coombes, who had listened with fascination.

'Oh, yes,' Lestrade told him. 'And some decent Jewish tailoring as well. Not like the rubbish they try to flog you these days!'

'No,' said Coombes patiently, 'I mean I never knew my old man tried to sell you no knocked-off suit and you lagged 'im.'

'Well,' said Lestrade, 'it isn't exactly the sort of thing you'd want to boast about, now is it?'

'No, I suppose not.' Coombes took a pull at his beer, and regarded the glass sadly.

'And now it's you,' said Lestrade. 'Like father, like son, eh, Frankie?'

Coombes shrugged his frail shoulders under his threadbare jacket. 'No use crying over spilt whatsit, is there?' he said. 'You got me to rights, Mr Lestrade, and I'll just 'ave to take what's due to me. Mind you,' he added, regarding the detective closely, 'I 'ear that you've got a little spot of bother yourself, isn't that right?'

'Now, how did you know that?' Lestrade asked.

'Oh, you 'ear these things,' and Coombes waved a hand grandly, as if to indicate that the editor of the *Times* dropped in frequently with the latest society gossip.

'Well, that's neither here nor there,' and Lestrade too lapsed into a gloomy silence.

Perhaps emboldened by this … or perhaps it was just the beer talking … Coombes went on, 'That so-and-so Clayton, wasn't it?'

Lestrade's only response was a cross between a shrug of the shoulders and a shake of the head.

'I knew him,' said Coombes, unexpectedly. 'Went to school with 'im, didn't I? We was next-door neighbours, as you might say.'

'Oh?' This was clearly news to Lestrade, and had the effect of dispelling his gloomy mood at once. 'I never knew that.'

'Oh, yes. When we was nippers, like, before all that trouble. 'E'd moved away from the street by that time.'

'And how did he strike you?' asked Lestrade.

'Strike me? Well, he was a rum cove, and that's a fact. You know. Odd.'

'That word again,' Lestrade said, looking at Holmes. '"Odd", that's how he struck everyone.'

'In what did this oddity consist?' Holmes asked Coombes curiously.

'Eh? Oh, I see.' Coombes considered. 'Well, he was sly, no, not sly, what's the word?'

'Secretive?'

'You 'ave it, Mr 'Olmes. Secretive, that's him to a "T", all right. Mark my words,' he told Lestrade, 'there was somethink that never come out at the trial.'

'Oh?' Lestrade sat bolt upright. 'And what might that have been, then?'

Coombes shrank back in his seat. 'I don't know that, do I? I mean, I hadn't got nothink to do with any of that. Only, I know there'll have been somethink, somewhere, see?'

'Oh.' The bitter disappointment was palpable in Lestrade's tone. He tapped Coombes's empty glass, and raised an eyebrow.

'Yes, please, Mr Lestrade. It's very kind ...' but Lestrade had gathered up the glasses and was striding through the door to the bar.

'Tell me,' said Holmes, 'this "something" that you say never came out at the trial, what did you mean by that?' and he gazed hard at Coombes.

Coombes shrugged. 'I don't know, like I told the inspector. But he'll have somethink, mark my words. Clayton, I mean. It was his nature, so to speak. You follow?'

'But what sort of thing?' Holmes persisted.

Another shrug, then a glance round the room, and, in a low voice, 'Bodies, like as not!' and Coombes gave a finer shudder than ever I saw on the professional stage.

'But the police searched his lodgings, as I understand it?'

'His lodgings! I arsk you!' Coombes sneered. 'It wouldn't be there, would it? Whatever it was?'

Holmes shot a look at me, and I recalled Lestrade's description of Clayton's rooms as being almost clinically clean. Was this the reason, then? Might there be some clue hidden elsewhere?

My thoughts were interrupted by Lestrade, who returned and slapped full glasses on to the table top.

'Lestrade, a word if you will?'

'Certainly, Mr Holmes.'

Holmes glanced significantly at Coombes, and Lestrade added, 'We'll be more private in the corner, there. Don't you think of running off without us, will you, Frankie?'

Coombes gave a sickly grin, and raised his glass to Lestrade in a hollow imitation of good fellowship. The three of us moved a short way off, but I noticed that Lestrade kept a sharp eye on his prisoner. 'Well, Mr Holmes?' said he.

'It's this way, Lestrade. I think this little contretemps might yet be of some use.' Lestrade looked puzzled, as I confess was I. Holmes went on, 'What have you against this fellow, Coombes?'

'Well, sir, there's the robberies that MacDonald spoke of; and that little matter earlier today.'

'H'mm. Some of the robberies were nothing special, though?'

'Mostly just rubbish taken, Mr Holmes, like I told you. One or two pieces of value, though.'

'You see, Lestrade, it occurred to me that this Coombes, being an old acquaintance of Clayton's, as it were, might perhaps gain his confidence, learn something of use from him?'

Lestrade looked sceptical. 'In return for ...'

Holmes nodded.

'The Yard would never wear it, Mr Holmes.'

'It is not the Yard's decision, Lestrade. It is entirely up to you.'

'And the other little matter, sir?'

I cut in, trying desperately to keep my voice level, 'Mr Holmes would scarcely wish it to be generally known that his pocket has been picked by the most unlikely, unsuccessful criminal in London!'

Holmes's look would have melted the largest glacier in Iceland, but he said merely, 'No great harm was done, after all. Save, perhaps, to my reputation!' he added, with a laugh.

'I dunno.' Lestrade was still unconvinced. 'It's a bit irregular. More than a bit.'

'Come, Lestrade,' I urged him, 'it is surely worth a try? Arrest this fellow now, and you gain some kudos, true, but think of what you might gain if you get his co-operation.'

Lestrade stood up, determinedly. 'I'll do it.' He marched across to Coombes, who looked up in some apprehension. ''Ave you still got them good bits that you pinched?' he demanded.

'Still got 'em, Mr Lestrade? I should think I 'ave!' Coombes laughed, mirthlessly. 'Couldn't get rid, could I?'

'Oh? But they were valuable pieces, as I recall?'

'They was too valuable. The fence said he daredn't touch 'em.'

Holmes frowned. 'I cannot believe that any receiver would turn down a decent profit. Where did you offer them, then?'

'Oh, a slop shop in Limehouse,' said Coombes vaguely.

Lestrade shook his head sadly. 'Hasn't a clue, has he? Mr Holmes, this other notion of yours. I'm not sure ...'

Holmes waved him to silence. 'Mr Coombes, could you lay your hands on the more valuable of the pieces that you have, ah, acquired?'

Coombes looked at Lestrade for a moment, then nodded.

Holmes went on, 'Inspector Lestrade here has it in mind to be lenient. Provided the goods are returned to his satisfaction, neither he nor I will press any charges against you.'

Coombes took a moment to work this out, then began, 'God bless you, gents ...'

'However,' said Holmes, 'there is one small favour we would wish in return.'

'Oh.' Coombes fell silent.

'We would wish you to ingratiate yourself with Clayton.'

'Ingrate? Oh, I see. Get chummy, like?'

'You could do that?' asked Holmes.

Coombes thought a moment. 'Yes,' said he, 'I could do it.'

'You might perhaps draw on your old friendship, or say that you can fully sympathize with his predicament, having yourself had some difficulty with the police? I am sure you will readily think of other openings.'

'Oh, yes. Rely on me, Mr 'Olmes.' Coombes broke off as the door opened, and someone came into the room.

I glanced round, and saw Inspector MacDonald. He stood there, turning his hat in his hands in some evident embarrassment.

Lestrade nodded to him. 'Sent to fetch me, is that it?'

MacDonald said, 'I fear that's so, Inspector. I had a most uncomfortable time with the chief, and the upshot was he sent me to scour all London for you, if need be.'

'I expected as much,' said Lestrade. 'I'll be right with you.' He glanced at Coombes, and then said to Holmes, 'I'm not sure about Frankie here, Mr Holmes. 'Clayton's new friends are a bit different from those he knew in the old days. Frankie here ... well, no offence, old son, but there are some high-class ladies hanging round him now, and I just don't know how you'd blend into that sort of company.'

'Don't give it a thought, Mr Lestrade,' said Coombes with confidence. 'I don't have no trouble in that direction.'

'No?'

'Not me. I get my share.'

'You astound me,' said Lestrade. 'The women of London just went down badly in my estimation!'

Holmes cleared his throat noisily. 'Be all this as it may,' said he, 'have we reached some agreement here?'

Lestrade nodded, and looked at Coombes, who nodded in his turn and said, 'I'm your man, sir.' He hesitated, then added, 'Er ... only thing is, having got alongside him, like ...'

'Well?'

'Well, sir, what I am to do then?'

'You are to keep your eyes and ears open,' said Holmes, 'and your mouth shut. You will report anything that you think might be of interest to Inspector Lestrade here, or to me. We may both be reached at number 221B Baker Street. Can you remember that?'

Coombes nodded again, then frowned.

'What is it now?' asked Lestrade.

'Well, where do I find him? 'Ow do I make myself known, like?'

Lestrade knotted his brow. 'Mr Holmes?'

'It must look accidental, I agree,' said Holmes.

MacDonald, who had been listening to this exchange in some bewilderment, now cleared his throat.

'Ah,' said Holmes, 'Mr Coombes here is to help us, if he can, with the Clayton affair. He is to be our man in the enemy camp, so to speak. The problem, Inspector, is how to introduce him into that enemy camp.'

'You want him to meet Clayton by accident, then? There's no difficulty there,' said MacDonald. 'He's in the habit of calling into a little public, of an evening, on his own. Probably by way of an antidote to his fancy friends.'

'You are certain?' asked Holmes.

'I told you I'd had him watched, and that was one thing my man spotted.'

'Capital! You can give Mr Coombes the details, and leave the rest to him.'

'Cut along then, Frankie,' Lestrade told him, when MacDonald had supplied the necessary information. 'I'll be round later to pick up those bits and pieces.' His gaze followed Coombes as the little man left the pub. 'Now, gents,' Lestrade went on, 'I feel like celebrating. We may not have reached the end of the tunnel, but at least we seem to be moving towards the light. It's good to be doing something, even if comes to nothing in the end. So, I'm buying the drinks.'

MacDonald coughed. 'I can only do so much,' he complained, 'or I'll be in hot water with the chief myself.'

Holmes consulted his watch. 'I would not wish to be churlish, Lestrade, nor yet to hold up the due workings of the law, MacDonald, but there was that other little matter I mentioned.'

Lestrade and MacDonald both looked puzzled.

Holmes sighed. 'In your very natural excitement at possible developments in the Clayton case, Lestrade, you have apparently forgotten that I promised you something that might have a bearing on the problem of Sir Octavius. You can come along too, MacDonald, for I think you will find it of interest. If you are quite ready, gentlemen?'

Eight

Lestrade and I followed Holmes up the stairs to our rooms in Baker Street. In his usual infuriating way, Holmes had refused to respond to any of our questions on the walk from Trafalgar Square. MacDonald was still merely puzzled, but Lestrade and I were growing increasingly restive. I could not say exactly what Lestrade was thinking, although his face spoke volumes, but I knew that if I were kept in the dark much longer, I would not answer for Holmes's continued safe existence.

On the landing, we encountered Billy, who told us, 'A visitor, Mr 'Olmes. A ... lady,' and there was a definite pause before the last word.

Holmes patted the boy on the head, and told him to fetch some tea. Billy did not respond at once, but stayed outside the room and regarded us curiously until we had gone through the door, so that I wondered just who our visitor might be.

The lady who sat in the armchair before the fire was certainly striking in appearance. Her long chestnut hair framed a face that fell just short of classical beauty, and which attracted at first sight less because of her features than because of the merry, albeit rather cynical, twinkle in her eye. She half rose as we entered, but Holmes waved her back to her chair, saying, 'Do not trouble, I beg you.' Without pausing to remove his coat, he went on, 'You have seen him?'

'As close as I am to you.' The voice was low and musical, but there was a slight accent of the East End which accounted for Billy's hesitation in his description. Still, I thought her far more attractive than many a 'lady' with formal claim to the title.

'And?' asked Holmes.

She shook her head, causing the hair to swirl around. 'Never. It was very like him, but it wasn't him. And he never recognized me.'

'Well,' said Holmes, 'I am sure he could never have mistaken you for another!' He rang the bell, and Billy appeared so fast that I suspected he had been lurking on the very threshold. 'Never mind the tea, Billy,' said Holmes, scribbling on a piece of paper. 'Now, you know where my brother, Mr Mycroft Holmes, lodges? Good. You are to take this lady there, at once. If my brother is not there, and he will almost certainly not be there, you are to stay with her until he arrives, and then give him this note. Do you understand that?' And he bowed low over the lady's hand, and ushered her out after the puzzled Billy.

When the door had closed after them, Holmes threw his coat on a peg, and said, 'I am sure she will be safe with Mycroft. Despite his appearance, he is a better boxer than I, and a heavier weight at that; moreover, he is an expert in the Japanese art of sumo, and has given lessons to the famous Mr Barton-Wright, who has, I see, lately invented his own system of self-defence under some fancy name.' He threw back his head and laughed aloud. 'For all that, I should like to see Mycroft's face when he reads my note! I have asked him to keep the lady at his lodgings for a while. It will all be proper enough, for he has a spare room and an aged and respectable landlady, but I guarantee he will never dare to close his eyes as long as she stays there.' He added, inconsequentially, 'Mrs Hudson will bring the tea in a moment, I am sure,' and wandered to the mantelshelf.

I picked up my heaviest walking stick. 'Holmes,' said I, 'this is intolerable!'

Lestrade laughed. 'Come, Mr Holmes, you go too far.'

Holmes picked up an old Dublin briar, and sat down. 'That lady,' said he, 'and we need not bandy her name about, has a rather curious profession, a profession which the convoluted divorce laws have brought into existence. She provides "evidence" in cases where a couple wish to separate, but have no grounds.' He looked at us, a smile on his face. 'No? Well then, I asked her to be at a certain place today, a place where I knew that Sir Octavius would also be. I asked her to see if she recognized him, or he her. As you heard, there was no recognition in either direction.'

'What the devil has that to do with the murder of Sir Octavius' wife?' asked Lestrade bluntly.

'Oh, nothing whatever. But it has everything to do with the murder of his brother, some ten years ago.'

'Oh!' cried Lestrade. 'The Brighton alibi.'

Holmes nodded, a smile of satisfaction on his face. 'The lady had been told that Sir Octavius wanted a divorce, you see, and she agreed to provide the evidence. She met Sir Octavius at Brighton, they spent the night at some hotel, doubtless playing cards, which is, so I am given to understand, the invariable custom in these cases, and in the morning she pocketed her fee and went on her way. In response to the enquiries made by the police, she replied, truthfully enough, that she had spent the night with Sir Octavius. She was asked to describe him, and she did so. They had ensured that there was sufficient likeness to pass, of course.'

'Only it wasn't him,' said Lestrade.

'Only it wasn't him. Now, I do not know how you plan to act in the matter of the wife's death, but perhaps you could bring in the lawyer who provided the alibi in that instance, tell him that Sir Octavius is certainly guilty of murdering his brother, and ask if the lawyer would like to change any small details of his testimony? And again, if you were to tell Sir Octavius that someone, and of course you need not specify just who it was, has betrayed him, perhaps he would draw the wrong conclusion, and then you would also solve the little puzzle of the lawyer's wife's death? Will that serve to …' But Lestrade was already on his way out, with MacDonald close on his heels.

'Well done, Holmes!' I told him. I reached for the decanter. 'I feel disinclined to wait for the tea. Will you join me?'

'I think perhaps I shall. A modest celebration might be indicated, as you say.' Holmes took the glass I offered, then frowned. 'Of course, none of this will help with the Clayton business, but it will reduce the amount of work Lestrade must do to clear his name. And now we will be able to concentrate all our efforts on the one problem.'

'By the way, Holmes, I did not like to say as much before him, but do you think this Coombes chap will be quite safe? Whatever the rights and wrongs of the Clayton case, his friends are a fast set, and little Coombes is so very guileless.'

Holmes's grip tightened on the stem of his pipe. 'He is under my orders,' said he, 'and consequently under my protection. If any harm comes to him ...' and he started as the pipe stem suddenly snapped in his fingers. 'Damnation!' He put the pieces carefully on a tray. 'Never mind, I can get it repaired.'

'You might ask them to clean it at the same time,' said I. 'That is, unless removing all the cake will cause what pathetic remnants are left of the bowl to disintegrate entirely.'

Holmes regarded the wreckage ruefully. 'It is past its best, I allow,' said he, 'but I shall instruct them to take special care. It is an old friend, and I value my old friends, such as this, yourself, and Lestrade. For that reason, I would wish to help him if it were at all possible.' He stood up and chose another pipe before going on, 'For the moment, though, we must wait in patience until Lestrade concludes this matter of Sir Octavius.'

We had not long to wait, as events turned out. Lestrade was back around six o'clock, with a slight roll in his gait, and a hint of whisky and cigar smoke about his person, all of which to my keen eye hinted at some modest and well-deserved celebration.

'Well?' said I.

Lestrade nodded with some satisfaction, and handed me a cigar. 'Very well, Doctor! Done up like a kipper,' he told us. 'All thanks to you, Mr Holmes. They're singing louder than old Wilson's canaries, and that's saying something. Calling each other all the names under the sun, the pair of them.' He threw his coat in the general direction of a peg, and sank into an armchair with a grateful sigh.

'And your superiors, how have they taken it?' Holmes wanted to know.

Lestrade's brow clouded slightly. 'The superintendent, he was all right. In fact, if it was up to him, I think the other business would've been all forgotten. The assistant commissioner, though, he's another kettle of fish altogether. Plays by the rules, he does.' He extended his hand, palm vertical, and shook it from side to side. 'Just like this, he is. First one way, then the other. "A good job, Lestrade", says he. But then, "There's still the other matter", he goes on.' He paused.

'Are you back on duty, though?' I asked.

Lestrade nodded. 'But with orders not to rock the boat, so to speak. I'm to keep out of the way as much as may be. Well, that suits me, just at the moment.'

'So, you have the credit for the arrest of Sir Octavius,' said Holmes, 'and you have recovered some stolen property, although there has been no arrest there. All that remains, then, is to wait until Mr Coombes should make his report.'

Now, I may say that this was easier said than done. The two of them were in excellent spirits for the rest of that evening, and indeed we had our own modest celebration, the three of us. But by next morning a kind of nervous reaction had set in, and both Holmes and Lestrade began to fret, wondering aloud if Coombes had made contact, and, if so, what the outcome might have been. In vain I protested that it was far too soon to expect any results; I added that even if Coombes had become bosom friends with Clayton on sight the previous evening, still Clayton might never say anything that would be of use. Lestrade regarded me venomously as I made this point.

'It's no good your looking like that,' I told him. 'The fact remains that Clayton might be innocent, and thus not have any guilty secrets to reveal.'

I will spare you Lestrade's reply; but I caught the look in Holmes's eye, and I knew that the same thought had occurred to him.

I put up with it as long as I decently could, then went off to my club where I spent the rest of the day. The evening was no better. Both men picked morosely at perfectly good food, and went off to bed at a ridiculously early hour, leaving me to my own thoughts, which were none too charitable.

The next day they were both still in very low spirits, and I found that I simply could not face them. I could have visited the club again, but I had recalled what the reader will by this time perhaps have forgotten, namely that I had intended to pursue some small enquiries of my own. Accordingly, I got Lestrade on his own, and asked him for the address of the refreshment rooms run by his old friend, Bessie. He looked rather askance at my question, for I suspect he feared some joke in poor taste on my part, but I convinced him to answer, and then bade him good day, leaving him looking after me with a mystified look upon his face.

The little cafe was on the Embankment, at no great distance from Scotland Yard, and I could see that Lestrade, and indeed his professional colleagues, might find it handy after the day's work. It was mid-morning when I looked in, and the place was quiet. A lady who corresponded to Lestrade's rather coarse description was dusting the zinc counter, and looked up as I entered.

I removed my hat. 'Ah! Have I the honour of addressing Mrs, or Miss, ah ... Bessie?' said I.

She regarded me with some degree of suspicion. 'Maybe. And who might you be, then?'

'I am a good friend of Inspector Lestrade,' I told her.

Her face cleared at once. 'Oh, that's different.' Her brow clouded again. ''Ere, 'e's not in no trouble, is 'e?'

'The fact is, madam, that he is,' I said. 'The Clayton case of twenty years back. You will perhaps have seen some account in the newspapers?'

She shook her head. 'I'm not much of a reader. But I did hear something about it.'

'Yes, Inspector Lestrade has come in for a good deal of criticism for his handling of the matter,' I went on. 'I, and some of his other friends, are naturally anxious to do what we can to help him. And I am sure that you yourself would wish to help, if at all possible?'

'Yes, of course. But what could I do, sir?'

'Do you recall the original case, at all?'

She nodded. 'Not in any detail, so to say. But I recall he was in a tizzy over it, him and his pals at the Yard.'

'He did not discuss it with you, though?'

Bessie shook her head. 'He wouldn't, would he?'

'No, I suppose not.'

'I know he had a bit of bother at the time,' added Bessie, with every sign of wanting to help. 'Him and his wife … well, I won't tell tales, but there was a bit of trouble there. You'll know what I mean, sir? And that upset him, never mind the murders and all.'

'Yes. Well,' said I, putting my hat back on my head, 'I'm sorry to have taken up your time. I did think it was a remote possibility, but the poor chap is in such a pickle that anything was worth a try.'

'You tell him I was asking after him, would you, sir? And tell him not to be a stranger.'

'I will indeed.'

'And if you are ever this way yourself, and fancy a cup of tea and a chat, please drop in.'

'I will remember,' I promised.

I went on then to my club, and spent an hour or so there, taking luncheon and playing billiards with some acquaintances. I had arranged with Mrs Hudson to be back at Baker Street for afternoon tea, so that it did not look as if I were avoiding Holmes and Lestrade altogether, and I set off back at about three o'clock. I had just turned the corner into Baker Street when I spotted Coombes, lounging along like any common idler. He looked directly at me, but gave no sign of recognizing me, so I understood that I was to pretend indifference, and did so.

As I reached him, he touched his greasy cap and waved an old clay pipe under my nose, as if begging a light. I handed him a vesta, and as he lit his pipe he muttered, not the usual thanks, but the cryptic message, 'Meet the grim reaper, eight tonight,' then with another tug at his cap he was gone.

Lestrade confirmed that The Grim Reaper was a low public house in the East End, and both he and Holmes cheered up very considerably at my news. I did not bother to report my morning's fruitless investigations, although I resolved to pass Bessie's good wishes on to Lestrade when the moment should be more opportune.

At half past seven we entered the public house, all suitably dressed in our oldest clothes, for Lestrade had told us that this was 'no place to go looking like a toff,' a sentiment which I echoed as I walked through the door to be met by a sort of tidal wave of noise, stale beer, perspiration, rank tobacco smoke and even less pleasant odours. We attracted no special attention, though, and promptly at eight the spare figure of Coombes slid into a seat next to us.

'Brought us a long way from home, Frankie,' complained Lestrade.

'Sorry, Mr Lestrade, but I thought it safer.'

'Quite right,' said Holmes. 'I gather you have some news for us?'

Coombes nodded, almost too excited to speak.

'That's quick work,' I said. 'You had no difficulty making Clayton's acquaintance, obviously?'

'Went like clockwork,' said Coombes. 'Bumped into him, accidental like, in the pub, and Bob's your uncle. Asked me back to his place, 'e did. Though it's not his, really, some of his friends are putting him up, but I met 'em, and they asked me to stay as well. My own room, and everythink.'

Lestrade looked sceptical. 'Get on all right with them, then, Frankie?'

'I knew one or two of 'em, as you might say,' said Coombes unexpectedly. He mentioned one or two names, Lady This, Sir Charles That.

'I wouldn't have thought they was friends of yours,' said Lestrade, even more sceptical.

'Oh, not friends, Mr Lestrade. Not as such. Friends of friends, you might say.' Coombes flushed.

'Oh, I get it. Your old pals have turned over some of their gaffs, that it, Frankie?'

'Mr Lestrade!'

'Interesting though these social notes are,' said Holmes, 'we might perhaps get to the real business of the evening?'

Coombes nodded assent. 'He's meeting a bloke tomorrow,' he told us. 'What sort of bloke?' asked Lestrade.

'A toff. Short, tubby. Well-dressed. Looks as if he might be the Lord Mayor or somethink,' said Coombes.

'I know the Lord Mayor, and it is not he,' said Holmes.

'Well, an Alderman or somethink of that, then. A toff.'

'You did not catch his name?'

Coombes shook his head. 'I wasn't supposed to see him, I don't think. I just caught the tail-end of what they were saying. "Tomorrow, at the bank, at noon", Clayton was saying. This other bloke, he wasn't too happy about it, but Clayton insisted.'

'H'mm. It could not have been "The Bank", I suppose, as in Bank of England?' asked Holmes.

Coombes shrugged.

'It is a pity you did not get his name,' said Lestrade.

'Oh, I forgot. He'd left his bag on the table outside in the 'all, a dispatch case, d'you call it? I took a look in there.'

'Old habits die hard, eh?' said Lestrade.

'You did well,' said Holmes, looking at the detective severely. 'It was a grave risk, but you did not flinch from it.'

Coombes looked pleased at this.

'What was in the bag?' Holmes went on.

'Just some papers.'

'Any names on them, then?'

Coombes shuffled uncomfortably in his seat.

Lestrade lowered his voice. 'It's this way, Mr Holmes,' said he, 'Frankie here ... well, he don't read any too well.'

'Ah. Forgive my obtuseness, Mr Coombes. I intended no offence.' Holmes's voice was bland, but his eye showed a suppressed anger at being so easily frustrated.

'But some of them 'ad a ... a motto, kind of thing,' said Coombes, taking a grubby scrap of paper from his pocket, 'and I drew it, best as I could.'

111

He laid the paper down on the table, and we saw a rough sketch of what was clearly intended to be a crest of some sort. I confess it meant nothing to me, and Lestrade too shook his head. But Holmes took a pencil from his pocket, altered a line here, and added another there, then sat back.

'Why,' said I, 'it is the sign of one of the private banks in Lombard Street.'

Holmes nodded. 'You have really done very well,' he told Coombes. 'Yes, Watson, it is one of the private banks in Lombard Street. Very small, very exclusive. And, more to our purpose, it has only the one branch in the City, the other I believe is in Harrow.'

'And what the devil is someone like Clayton doing with a small, exclusive private bank?' Lestrade wanted to know.

'That's it, isn't it?' said Coombes. When we looked blank, he added, 'That's where he's hid it. And this other bloke, he's the manager, like as not. I said he was a toff, didn't I?'

'"It"?' said Holmes.

'Yes, "it", what I was telling you about. Whatever "it" is that he's hidden. The clue, like.'

'Whatever "it" may be, we can surely not afford to neglect this opportunity,' said Holmes. 'Noon, tomorrow, you say? Well, we shall be there, I think. Lestrade?'

The detective nodded. 'Hang on, though, what if it's the other branch, Harrow, did you say?'

'H'mm. I think it unlikely,' said Holmes, 'but we must stop all the earths, I agree. Look here, MacDonald knows Clayton by sight, so he can cover the Harrow branch.'

'And what is he to do?' asked Lestrade.

'Why, just we will do. Use his eyes, and his imagination, and act accordingly. We can give him no other advice, for I freely confess I have no idea as to what may happen tomorrow.'

Nine

We were in Lombard Street and across the road from the bank at eleven next morning. Lestrade had insisted upon our being early, and Holmes had not demurred, saying that it was better safe than sorry. I ventured to make some mild protest, saying that Clayton and his new friend had arranged a time, that their meeting was fixed for when the bank was at its busiest and they would thus attract no attention, and thus they would be unlikely to vary it, but I had been unable to resist the combined efforts of the other two.

That they were right and I was wrong, that the precaution was justified was proved when, at half past eleven, a carriage swept up to the entrance to the bank, and Clayton and another man, whom I recognized only as the 'stout, tubby' personage of Coombes's description, alighted.

'Cunning devil!' said Lestrade, digging me in the ribs by way of reproach.

'Have you got your forces in place?' asked Holmes, as the two men went through the great double door of the bank, the uniformed commissionaire snapping to attention as they passed him.

'A half dozen constables round the corner, sir,' answered Lestrade, holding up a police whistle. 'Though I can't see as these two will give us much trouble,' he added scornfully.

'What exactly do you intend?' I asked him curiously.

'Why, to see what he's up to.'

'And if it proves to be all above board? If this is all some further grotesque misunderstanding? What then, Lestrade?'

Lestrade gave a defensive shrug of the shoulders. 'What is it you racing men say, Doctor, "double or quits", is it?'

'More like "make or break", I should think,' said I.

Lestrade looked hard at me, then grinned, nodded, and shook my hand. 'Make or break it is, gents,' said he, moving to cross the road as Clayton and the other man emerged from the bank.

The other man was making as if to get back into the carriage, and since he had no means of knowing us, he took no notice as we approached. But Clayton stopped dead in his tracks, and if ever I saw naked fear and guilt on a man's face, I saw it then. He was holding a bulky package in his hands, and he strove unsuccessfully to conceal it as Lestrade reached him.

'And what have we here, then, Algernon?' asked Lestrade, indicating the package.

The other man had now realized that all was not well. 'What is this?' he asked in a pompous manner. 'Who are you?'

'Police,' said Lestrade shortly. 'And I'll thank you to hand over that package,' he told Clayton.

They blustered, but to no avail, although in the end Lestrade had pretty well to snatch the package from Clayton. He broke the wax seal, and took out a sheaf of photographs. He glanced at one or two with a look of horror, before handing them to me.

I looked at the pictures in my turn. I will not dwell on their subject matter, other than to say that it was a manifestation of some perverted intellect. Murder is one thing, gratuitous mutilation another, but to photograph the end result is yet a third. Perhaps some of my modern German alienist colleagues will find the right words, but I cannot. I can only say that I have seldom seen such vileness, such clear evidence of evil, in all my life. I gave a grimace, and was about to return the photographs to Lestrade, when something struck me. I looked again at the pictures.

'You mentioned five boys, Lestrade?' said I.

'Well, Doctor?'

'There are six here.'

He fairly tore the photographs from my extended arm, and went through them, muttering under his breath. At the third picture, he stopped, and something like triumph shone in his eye. 'This is the first one,' he told us. 'The one we thought was different, the one that Algernon here was never tried for.'

Clayton's face turned a sickly green ... I use the description literally ... and he slumped against the wall of the bank for support.

'Yes, you ...' said Lestrade, and the epithet, foul as it was, seemed to me to be entirely justified, 'yes, you swine, you'll hang for that one, even if I can't touch you for the rest. And you, too,' he added to the stout man.

'Do you know who I am?' asked the stout man. He waved a hand to indicate the bank behind him. 'I am the chairman of ...'

'I don't care who you are,' Lestrade told him, 'you're involved with this creature here, and that's good enough for me.'

Clayton had by this time recovered some of his composure, and he waved a hand feebly. 'Nothing to do with him,' he told Lestrade. 'Just kept my package safe. Never knew what was in it.'

The stout man nodded agreement to this. Lestrade looked baffled. 'Well,' said he, 'I have the man I set out to get, if nothing else. That'll do to be going on with.'

'You may have more,' said Holmes calmly. He touched the edge of the top photograph. 'The surface is highly glazed, you see. It will take finger marks of almost textbook perfection.'

Lestrade looked a question at him.

'The package was sealed,' Holmes went on. 'There will naturally be the finger marks of yourself, Inspector, and Doctor Watson here, and presumably Mr Clayton. If there are also the marks of our other friend here ...'

The fact that the stout man slid to the ground in a dead faint told its own story at this point. Lestrade blew his police whistle.

'This, I think, must be the third man of whom a witness spoke,' said Holmes, regarding the inert form upon the pavement with some interest. 'It seems there was honour among thieves, of a sort, for none of them would implicate the others, unless it were out of their hands. Even in the worst specimens of humanity, the lowest of the low, there may yet be something approaching a spark of decency, you see.'

'Maybe,' said Lestrade. 'But it won't cut much ice with a judge and jury. And none at all with the hangman!'

In the event, he was right.

Ten

'A nasty business, Holmes,' I ventured.

Holmes, who had scarcely spoken to me all morning, nodded. 'It was certainly that, Watson. I have had some dismal cases, but this must go down as one of the worst. A salutary reminder that our chosen profession is not always wholesome, not always a matter of helping a beautiful young duchess find a missing silver spoon. There were not even any of those scintillations of humour which so enliven some of your accounts, my boy.'

'As you say, it is in the nature of our business. Why, any young bobby on his first day alone on the beat might run into murder of the most sordid kind, vice of the foulest description. How much more likely is it then that two old hounds like us must occasionally encounter unpleasantness? It was not a total failure, Holmes. At least you caught the villains.'

'That is true enough. A success, of sorts. But at what cost? Two men's lives. Two more lives to add to the tally. And will their deaths accomplish anything? I wonder.'

'I should put that in the credit, and not the debit, column, Holmes!' I told him. 'You and I did not commit those horrific crimes, after all, nor did Lestrade. And neither did we incite or encourage the rogues who did. If nothing else, many a wretched woman in the East End will sleep easier knowing that her child is safe. To say nothing of having saved

Lestrade's good name. I see it as nothing less than a triumph. And I am certain that Lestrade will tell you the self-same thing. Indeed, I fancy you will not have to wait long to hear him say it, for that, unless I am much mistaken, is Lestrade ringing the bell of the street door.'

'Amazing!' said Holmes, recovering some of his usual good humour and gazing at me with open admiration. 'Even I would not venture to identify a visitor from the ringing of the bell.'

'Oh, it is nothing,' I answered modestly. 'Lestrade's ring is unmistakable. And besides,' I added truthfully, 'I ran into him in Oxford Street earlier this morning, and he said he would call.'

Before Holmes could work out a reply, Lestrade had entered the room with all his usual breezy cheerfulness. He carried a great sheaf of newspapers, which he threw onto the table, before shaking Holmes's hand warmly. 'I really cannot thank you enough, Mr Holmes,' said he. 'I thought I was a goner, for sure.'

'Ah, well, it all ended in a satisfactory enough fashion, I suppose,' said Holmes. He gestured at the newspapers. 'They carry the report of the arrest, or rather, "the reports of the arrests", I should say, for you have had a busy few days just lately?'

Lestrade nodded. 'They have changed their tune somewhat,' he said rather bitterly. 'But that was to be expected.'

'I should be grateful if you could leave the papers,' said Holmes. 'There are some details I would wish to record in my scrapbooks.'

Lestrade winked at me.

'No,' said Holmes, 'I am not that vain! I merely wished to take a note of the names of those misguided people who had supported Clayton initially.'

'And why that?' asked Lestrade, puzzled.

'It did not occur to you that the claims as to his innocence, and likewise the vilification of yourself, might have been organized?'

'Well, we know he had friends ... a peer of the realm with egalitarian notions, a clergyman who is always quick to forgive

118

villains, provided their villainy is directed against some third party and not himself, of course. Others, too, misguided, as you say, but nothing more, surely?"

Holmes shook his head impatiently. 'More than that, I fancy, Inspector. There was some organizing genius behind it, mark my words!'

'Oh!' said Lestrade, 'this is not about Professor Moriarty again, surely? Why, the man's been dead this ten years.'

'No man is more aware of that than I myself,' said Holmes calmly. 'But there were others. And there are still others. By striking at you, Lestrade, they hoped to strike at the whole of Scotland Yard, at the whole system of justice, perhaps even … indirectly … at me. So, with your permission, I shall just note their names, for future reference.'

Lestrade looked at me and winked again. 'He has his methods, Doctor! And, Lord knows, I have enough reason to be grateful, aye, and more than grateful for that. Make your notes, Mr Holmes, and if ever you decide the time is right to act, you know who to call upon.' He took the glass I offered him, and wiped his brow. 'Never was I more glad to see the end of a case, gents, and that's a fact. Still, it all came right in the end.'

'A sordid business, though, Inspector, I fear,' said Holmes, glancing up from his note-taking.

'Well, it wasn't the cleanest case I've ever known, and that's a fact,' said Lestrade. 'But remember, Mr Holmes, that it was none of my making, nor yours either, come to that. We simply cleared up the mess those villains had left.'

'Just what I said,' I told him.

'You are right, of course,' said Holmes.

'And the beauty of it is,' Lestrade went on, 'that now everything's back to normal, you and I will be able to work together on many a new case!'

'Brandy, Holmes?' said I.

"With five volumes you could fill that gap on that second shelf."
(Sherlock Holmes, *The Empty House*)

So why not complete your collection of murder mysteries from Baker Street Studios?
Available from all good bookshops, or direct from the publisher with free UK postage
& packing. To see full details of all our publications, range of audio books, and
special offers visit www.crime4u.com where you can also join our mailing list.

Baker Street Studios Limited, Endeavour House, 170 Woodland Road,
Sawston, Cambridge CB22 3DX
sales@baker-street-studios.com